WHEN SHE HOLLERS

Also by Cynthia Voigt:

CYNTHIA VOIGT
WHEN SHE HOLLERS

**SCHOLASTIC
HARDCOVER**

Scholastic Inc.
New York

Library of Congress Cataloging-in-Publication Data

Voigt, Cynthia.
When She Hollers / Cynthia Voigt.
p. cm.
Summary: Tish, a teenager who has been enduring abuse from
her adoptive stepfather since she was a small child, finally
decides she must do something to stop him.
ISBN 0-590-46714-X
(1. Child sexual abuse — Fiction. 2. Stepfathers — Fiction.)
I. Title.
PZ7.V874Wh 1994
(Fic) — dc20   93-43519
                                                      CIP
                                                       AC

12 11 10 9 8 7 6 5 4 3 2 1   4 5 6 7 8 9/9

Printed in the U.S.A.   37

First printing, September 1994

For Robin & Jessica & Merrilee —
First readers

WHEN SHE HOLLERS

—One—

She put the survival knife down on the table. It pointed across at him.

She couldn't breathe.

"From now on — " she said. "I'll have this knife." Her knees were watery, and her mouth trembled. "All the time." She sat down.

He was pretending not to hear. He poured milk from the carton into his cereal.

"You better — "

She swallowed.

" — listen — "

She pushed the reluctant words up out of her throat to stand in a row on the table, standing in a straight row facing him.

"You better believe — "

1

He looked up at her, looked down. Bored, for everyone to see.

"Or the bathroom, either," she said.

He rolled his eyes. *Is she crazy, or what?* his face asked.

Mom wasn't paying any attention. Mom was standing by the counter waiting for toast to pop up, so she could spread margarine on it and pile it up on a plate and then set the plate down on the table and watch all the hands grab, and then she'd take the empty plate back and put more slices of bread into the toaster. Breakfast was a busy time for Mom, getting everyone fed and out the door with packed lunches.

"You come in — ever again, and — " Tish made herself say that. "When I'm — " heart was beating in her ears, and beating.

Luley was listening, but Brad and Winny were fighting over something in Winny's hand. Luley was about to start laughing at Brad's eye-popping, head-wagging retard face — and maybe Luley would be all right, maybe because Luley was his own daughter.

"Or my bed!" Tish yelled that. "You hear me? You come near me and — "

His face got red. His ears, too. He couldn't ignore her now.

"Just what are you — ?" He pretended

he didn't know. His hands made fists on top of the table.

She hated his hands.

"I'll cut your hands off, I'll — "

She was standing up, leaning across the table at him.

" — saying. She doesn't know what she's saying, some kind of teenaged hysteria." He sounded like he didn't care, but he didn't take his eyes off her face. And he hated her for saying it.

" — cut your heart out I'll — cut your eyes out, cut you, I'll — "

His face was beet-red. Maybe he'd bust a gut right there.

Maybe some blood vessel in his brain would explode, and he'd fall down dead.

And she'd dance on his grave.

"She's lying," he growled, snarled. "She's a liar. We all know how you lie, Tish."

"I don't. I'm not." They didn't believe her. They didn't want to, any of them — as if they cared more about believing that she was a liar than about what was true. "It's true!" she cried out. "You know it's true! You know you do!"

Everyone was watching him now. He was half out of his chair now. She had the knife in her right hand, resting on the table. She leaned on the table. Luley was crying. Mom stood at the counter, facing away, shoulders hunched.

Tish was so scared — she was clutching on to her right shoulder, her left arm across her chest, so she wouldn't fly out of her own body — running away — leaving herself behind, and if she did that he could —

She held on tight.

His mouth spat saliva. "She's got some reason for this. She's up to something."

She hated his mouth; lips, teeth, and tongue. She hated him. Whenever she looked at him. And saw his hands. He said *Turn the light on* and whenever she looked at him she heard his voice saying *Turn the light on* and whenever she saw his hands she hated herself.

He pushed himself back down onto his chair.

Tish made herself keep looking at his face, and keep looking back at his measuring eyes.

She knew that look in his eyes and it made her sick, and she didn't know how to stop putting that look in his eyes. She thought she might as well go ahead and blow up into tears, and throw down the knife, and give up —

"Has somebody put you up to this?"

4

At the sound of his voice, his Daddy voice, Tish felt sick.

"How could you let somebody — turn you against me, Tish?"

She hadn't, she knew she hadn't, and *still* she almost believed him. She almost didn't hate him. She almost hoped he was the kind of crazy where you become another different person, an entirely different kind of person, the kind of person who could come into the bathroom —

Tish couldn't stand to remember —

and turn up the radio volume —

She didn't have to remember. If Tonnie was crazy, then he wouldn't remember, either, and what he was doing wasn't anything he *meant*. He just — couldn't help it, if he was crazy. No wonder he felt bad about what Tish was saying. Poor Tonnie, if he couldn't help it. Tish knew that if she would just admit she was wrong, and give up trying to have a fight with him —

"You used to love me best," Tonnie said sadly. Sometimes he just sounded so nice, nice the way he used to be, the way she used to think he was — like when he wanted her to have a room of her own so she would know she was special to him, his special daughter. "You've always been my special daughter," he said sadly.

5

Nice was scary. Which made no sense, so maybe she *was* crazy. Maybe she *was* lying.

— but if she gave up now, she'd have to give him the knife, and then she'd have no way to keep herself —

Nice was scarier than mean, with Tonnie. "No," she whispered. There was a scream in her belly, but the most she could say was to whisper it. "No."

"Bet I know, bet she's gotten herself pregnant, that boyfriend, that Kipper, he's kippered you, hasn't he, Tish." It wasn't a question. And his eyes were angry and had that look and now they were jealous, too.

She thought she would let the scream out. And never stop screaming. But if she did, they'd probably just say she was crazy.

At least then she could be locked safe away in some loony bin. When you were locked up you wouldn't find yourself hanging from a tree, dead, no matter how much you might want to. In a loony bin they wouldn't let you off yourself — and if she let the scream out, they'd probably send her to one. Maybe.

Or maybe not, maybe they'd just keep her inside this house all the time, forever, and she'd never get out at all. So she better not scream.

Her heart was jumping around in her chest, trying to run away.

"You're a lying slut."

Wasn't. Didn't.

"A pregnant," he leaned across the table, "lying, slut. Your mother at least was pretty enough to get your father to marry her. But Kipper'll leave you on your own, you and the baby." Tonnie liked that idea. "Abandon you."

Her legs were stiff, and her breath was jammed back down into her lungs because the pill was only ninety-eight percent sure. She'd been thinking there was no chance, but there was a chance. A two percent chance. Sometimes, Tonnie seemed to know about her. Sometimes, he knew things about her before she had any clue.

What if this was a time he was right?

Tish had thought she was as scared as she could be, but that wasn't true, now she was more scared. She left the outside skin of herself where it was, but she detached from it. She got herself loose from the outside skin of herself. The idea of being pregnant was like spikes set up all along the inside of the skin side of her. She shrank back inside of herself, a little person again, until she was crouching inside of herself with her back to the wall, listening to steps coming closer beyond the door there was no lock to. No bolt. No way to keep closed if someone knew you were in there hiding, listening to his footsteps when they stopped outside the door.

She could tell the truth. But she didn't know what would happen then. How bad things might get.

And what was the point of trying to fight with him? She knew what happened when she tried to fight with him, didn't she?

She knew exactly what happened. Maybe Tonnie was right, maybe she was just kidding herself, maybe what happened was exactly what she wanted to happen. Tonnie knew her inside and out, he knew how to make her do what he wanted. He knew what she was thinking and sometimes she even thought what he wanted.

If she knew what happened when she fought with him, and she went ahead and fought with him — Tish didn't know. She just didn't know. Sometimes she thought she *was* the piece of shit he said she was.

Even when she was little he'd tease her about that, about how if you rearranged the letters of her name you got shit; and she'd get all worked up and angry, and crying, and he'd be laughing, Mom'd be laughing, until she had to laugh herself at the way Tonnie'd say her name, Tish, out in public and she had to know the word he was thinking, what he was getting away with. It was their secret, until she was having such a good time, and it was so exciting when Tonnie got away with stuff — even though she wished he wouldn't, she wished he wouldn't say her name that laughing way.

He laughed now. "Why *should* I? I mean, look at yourself — your face is nothing much, and now those pimples and — your figure isn't much, it's nothing compared to your mother's — and your hair, you don't even try — your mother keeps in shape, she's in great shape, what would I want —?" he asked her, and everyone else. "How can you flatter yourself I'd even notice — ?"

She almost believed him, the way he was almost laughing, the way he reached out an arm and gathered Mom in, and held her close to him; and her mother smiling, a plate of toast in her free hand, Mom's other hand held inside his, both of these hands resting on her mom's pregnant belly.

Tish wanted to believe him.

If he was telling the truth and she was crazy, then everything made sense. Because then none of it had happened.

"You're a liar!"

She yelled it.

She shouldn't have yelled. You had to stay calm and not yell, and not cry, or nobody believed you. If you yelled or cried tears, nobody had to listen. Those were the rules.

He rolled his eyes. *Now what did I say?*

Her skin tightened all over her body, shrinking up stiff and tight with fear.

He just watched her.

Then Brad spilled his cereal bowl all over, and Tonnie slapped him and her mother said, "Go to your room." Winny laughed because Brad was in trouble, and Mom slapped him and said, "Go to your room." The two little boys raced away, to get to their room and close the door and turn the music on. Mom got paper towels to mop up the mess. Her mother was having another baby again.

"Help your mother, Luley," he said. Her stepfather. Tonnie.

Luley had tuned them all out and she was eating cereal and reading the back of the box, as if nothing much was happening, as if everything was normal.

Which it was, in a way. Except for the knife, everything was like always. The kind of breakfast that, if you could get anything down your throat, you had a stomachache after.

Thoughts crowded together into Tish's mind, so close she couldn't tell one from the other, not where one began and another left off, and they moved so fast, she couldn't catch them.

He wasn't lying about her looks, at least, she thought: she *wasn't* much to look at. Zits all over her face, and her tits were minuscule, and she had a pot, toothpick legs, her toes were long and bony and ugly, like her hands, broad hips, broad butt — she was a mess, pretty much, pretty much all of the time. Maybe Tonnie was right. Maybe she did want him coming after her, just like he said, maybe she always had. She could hear his voice, *Asking for it.* What he'd been saying for years, *It's your own fault.* His voice was much stronger and easier to believe than the little high whiny voice, from deep inside her where she was hiding curled up, whimpering. The little voice like some dying siren, some winding down wind-up siren. Saying it wasn't true what he was saying.

But it was like, whenever Tonnie started looking at her she got zits, some allergic reaction. He hated zits and made fun of them and talked about them and kept asking her what she was eating, and kept saying, "You know why you're getting pimples. I know what you've been doing." His thick tongue sweeping around his lips.

She didn't know. Except, whatever it was, it was shameful to her, it was so shameful that he enjoyed it.

All of this went through her mind as fast as a bird, just crossing her line of vision, like a flock of birds, rising, wheeling, gone — all the thoughts.

She'd asked Kipper about it and he had no idea what Tonnie was talking about. At least, that was what Tish concluded. She wasn't positive about it because she didn't dare ask even Kipper directly. She couldn't tell what Kipper would think, if he decided to think about it, if she asked him directly. She had to go sideways to ask, saying, "You know what they used to say about boys getting hairy palms?" Kipper laughed — as if there were no clouds in the sky, ever. There was only sunshine in Kipper's world. "Yeah, I know, babe. It's not true." He held out his hands, palms up.

"What about zits, Kip?" she'd asked.

"It's hormones, just hormones mounting up," he said. "When you get older, they pretty much go away. It's normal," he said, Kipper the big naturalist. "But *you* don't have — "

She kissed him so he wouldn't lie to her, and also so he couldn't look too closely at her, if he'd maybe missed her bad complexion. Kipper was an eyes-closed kisser. So if she didn't want him to see her, all she had to do was kiss him. She kissed him as well as she knew how, and then she pushed him away and walked off. "C'mon, Tish," she heard him say, "come back," and didn't turn around. If she turned around, she didn't know what he would see stamped on her face. Or peeping out of her eyes, she didn't know what he might do if he knew what she was really like.

It didn't used to be — she thought; she didn't used to be like this — but then she couldn't remember when that was. It was too long ago, long since —

She couldn't even picture her real dad. Who'd walked out before she was a year old. Because he only married her mom because she got pregnant with Tish. He walked out and went to work in Alaska, where chances of jobs were better, and the pay was better. And he got himself divorced and then who knew? The postcards to her mom stopped coming after that.

There had never been any checks, and then Tonnie adopted her and when she was adopted her dad didn't have to pay for her.

But still, he was her real dad.

Miranda had a real dad, didn't she? and a mom, too, until the mom died. And still there was Miranda, naked, hanging from a tree.

All these thoughts, flickering like birds, Tish couldn't tell what was true here.

Because the truth could make you free. Mrs. Wyse wrote that on the board, "The truth shall make you free." Maybe you had to know it first, maybe that was it, that was why . . .

but *free*

If Tish could be free — she could almost taste free, like ice on a hot day, cold and clear, not even needing flavor.

The taste of that word in her mouth, as if being afraid had sweated her dry but free washed her down cool inside, in her mouth and throat, belly and brain.

Free.

And the truth.

She knew the truth, whatever he lied and said.

The truth was still the truth, no matter how many people lied and said it wasn't.

She hoped.

Her body knew. Like the magician's girl who got put into a box and sawed in half. It was all a trick, without even blood, there were two girls, one with her legs up tight cramped against her chest and her head sticking out for everyone to see, and another doubled over her stomach and only her legs showing. Between them the place where the saw sawed through.

All this went through Tish's mind in a flash, like lightning, barely seen, then gone, and darkness already gathering up again.

They rolled the boxes with the two circus girls in them over to opposite sides of the stage. One box showed only the top half. One only the bottom half. Sawed into half, one smiling, smiling, and the other wiggling, wiggling toes and kicking ankles — two halves sawed apart and it didn't even hurt.

When Tish thought about it, she thought she'd forget about the survival knife, and all, and just wait for it to end because maybe it wasn't happening anyway after all.

She did lie, and she knew it. Just — she didn't think she was lying about what they said she was lying about. But if everybody said it was only a circus trick, not real, and if she could only be sure it really wasn't real . . .

Because when they forgot to put the second girl into the box, the saw went right though the only girl's belly. The saw had

15

serrated edges, little sharp teeth, and it sawed and sawed right through her stomach. And the girl couldn't make a sound. It took forever, a forever of being chewed apart. Because if she even started to make a sound . . . Everyone in the audience would hear, and know it wasn't a trick; everyone watching would know it was real.

That was worse than being sawed at. Anything was easier, anything, than that, no matter how bad. Anything had to be easier than telling the truth. Than thinking about the truth. Than trying to be free.

All this passed through her mind like music, like music with pictures, a video, passing quickly.

Pictures it made her sick to see. When he said *Turn the light on.*

She couldn't get any farther away inside from her skin. She couldn't get away.

Tonnie was spooning cereal into his mouth, her mother was making toast, Tish was standing there, and no time had gone by at all. It was still the same time. Luley got up, leaving her bowl on the table, and picked up her lunch box by the door and went out, to go to school.

Free, the truth shall make you free, *free.* Tish remembered the words written on the board in Mrs. Wyse's capital letters. She guessed Miranda was free now.

"Go to your room, Tish," Tonnie said to her. "I've got a couple of things to say to your mother, first." His tongue wiped his lower lip. "Then I'll deal with you."

Tish shook her head.

No.

He looked at his watch. He looked at her. He smiled. He wanted her in her room waiting. Waiting for him, and afraid. He hated her and he'd get even.

She didn't know where she got brave enough to shake her head No at Tonnie.

"I'll deal with you," he said again. "Sooner or later, and don't kid yourself otherwise. Later is fine by me. I like later better. When I get home from work. You can spend the day in your room," he said. "And think about what you just said here. And think about how I'm going to feel about it."

Tish shook her head again and she couldn't even swallow.

He ignored her. "I think I'd better be the one to deal with her," Tonnie said. "Don't you think so, Barbie? We can't have her going around saying things like — you never know what people will decide to believe, you can't ever tell — "

Tish had the knife in her hand.

"I won't," she muttered.

Tonnie turned back to face her, slowly. He was tall, and broad, heavy and muscled. "What — ?" he growled, snarled.

"Won't — " her voice squeaked. "Go to my room. I'm going to school."

"You . . . what?"

But he stayed there across the table. He was stronger, twice as big all over, across his shoulders and chest, around his arms, but he stayed there across the table, stayed still. She didn't know what she could do if he started to move.

She was sick of herself being so frightened all the time, and she felt sick. "I have to go to school. It's the law."

Tonnie didn't care about the law, as long as nobody caught him. "I'll sign your excuse," he said. "Parents have rights, too," he said, "in case you've forgotten, let me remind you of that. Parents still have a *few* rights left."

So *what* if he was going to hit her?

But it *hurt.*

So *what* if it hurt? One way and the other, he was going to hurt her and *so what*? What kind of baby was she, what kind of coward, chicken, deserved to be shoved into the box and sawed at, as if she really was two girls, and if she really couldn't ever —

"YOU CAN'T STOP ME FROM GOING

TO SCHOOL!'' she screamed. ''YOU CAN'T MAKE ME BREAK THE LAW!''

And Tonnie relaxed. She'd had him nervous, but not anymore now. Tish didn't understand him, didn't understand what was going on at all. She couldn't understand even when she tried.

Tonnie talked in his normal voice now, deep and strong, a voice you could trust, sort of amused but not ever disturbed by what was going on. What was going on was no more than little tiny waves up against his big strong toes. ''Why are you screaming at me like that? You don't need to scream at me, do you? Have I been going deaf? And my best friends won't tell me?''

He was teasing, the way he'd done when she was little, and she felt like giggling the way she had when she was a little girl, and Tonnie teased her to make her laugh and be happy, and tickled her until she couldn't help laughing. She knew he was teasing, because Tonnie didn't have any friends, or any best friend. He just had his family, that was all he wanted, he said.

''Can you make sense out of her, Barbie?'' he called. ''You were a girl, is this what girls are like at her age?''

Mom was at the sink. Mom didn't really turn around, she kind of shifted hands in the sink, keeping on washing, to look over her shoulder and not see anything. Then she shifted back to doing the dishes.

Mom wasn't listening, even if she could hear over the TV sounds. Tonnie spoke in a low voice. "At this point your mother might not be a match for you. But I am." He was quiet now, peaceful. "More than a match," he smiled. "As you know." There was music on the TV and music from the boys' room. All the mixed-together music muzzed in her ears. "Sit down," Tonnie said.

His fist balled up, and he had on one of his little mean smiles.

She sat. The survival knife was in her lap, across her legs.

He watched her.

She waited.

"You didn't eat one bite of breakfast," he said. He sounded concerned, like a concerned father on TV. "A good breakfast is important. Try a piece of toast, at least, your mother makes good toast." He lowered his voice again. "She worries when you won't eat, you know that, that you might get too thin, get sick, get that anorexia nirvana. Your mother worries about you."

The little smile said *he* knew better than to worry.

"Eat," he said.

The little smile said *he* knew what was good for her.

She didn't know what to do. She was afraid to obey, afraid what he'd think if she started obeying. She picked up a piece of toast and bit into it. She chewed on the bite — it had cooled down and had no flavor except a little margarine taste — until it seemed she'd been chewing on it too long.

Swallowing was the hard part, with Tonnie watching.

She put the toast down on her plate.

He winked. Friendly Man. Buddy Man. "Good girl," he said.

His hand was a fist on the table where she could see it.

"Now, let's get this clear. Just what is it you've taken it into your head to accuse me of doing? You can tell me."

She wasn't about to say *that* —

He winked again.

He wasn't winking, his hand wasn't a fist, she was just hysterical, is all. He was concerned, understanding, trying to understand, and worried about her.

"I'd like to help you," he said. "About that knife. Since you feel like you need to have it, to have a knife — you must feel afraid of something. What are you afraid of, Tish?"

She couldn't believe he was asking her that. When the screams rang up against the palm of his hand and he wouldn't let them get past.

"Tell me, Tish. You know — you can say anything to me."

She shook her head and clutched the knife. If he wanted her to say it, it must be that if she did, that would give him what he wanted. There was some reason, if he wanted her to say it.

"Barbie? Turn down the TV, you better hear this, too."

Her mother turned down the TV.

"You're having trouble saying it? I'll help, if I can," he said. Nice Man now, Daddy Man.

Her mother stayed by the sink, the water turned off, TV turned down. Her mother's back was hunched a little and her head bent over, protecting the baby in her stomach. Tish couldn't see her mother's face.

Tish had been as brave as she could. She had been braver than she thought she ever could be. And it wasn't going to be brave enough. She couldn't be brave enough. Not now. Not ever in her life.

Tonnie smiled.

"You were saying — stop me if I'm getting it wrong — as if I'd come into your room. Do you mean your bedroom?"

She nodded.

"At night?" His voice sounded mild and surprised, his hand was a fist, and his eyes wandered like hands across her shoulders and neck. "Are you saying that I come into your room at night?"

She nodded helplessly. It was the truth. But she couldn't believe it, the truth in his mouth. His mouth turned it into a lie.

Looking at his mouth made her sick.

"But, Tish, why would I *do* that?"

She wasn't going to say anything. She was trapped in the magician's table, locked into the box, crushed up against herself — and now he was wheeling her around, making her dizzy, to show everyone how honest he was. She began to see his trick now.

Her mother reached out and turned up the music again.

"Let me guess. Because I want to — what? See you with your clothes off? Your breasts, perhaps? Or more, are you saying I want to touch — "

His eyes had tongues that were licking at her, and she muttered, "Stop it! Stop that!" He was talking to get himself going and he liked making her listen and he liked it even

more when her mother was listening, too
— tricking her mother.

Tish threw the carton of milk into his face.

It hit his nose and mouth and poured all
over his front.

There was a long, silent minute, growing
bigger, within all the noise of music. Tish
and Tonnie were in a bubble of silence, and
all around music was so loud, nobody even
noticed the bubble. Nobody had to notice it
with the music so loud.

"That's it!" Tonnie rose up from the table.
"That's the end! I've had all I'm going to
take from you! I can tell you that! Promise
you!" He sounded like he was going to
really lose it, finally. Well, good, let him,
and she'd stick the knife into his arm, and
pull down on it with all of her weight.

He wiped at his face with a napkin, and
wiped at the front of his shirt. "If you think
that this kind of behavior — "

He wanted to grab her and take her to
her room, and close the door.

"Don't come near me," Tish said. She
wanted to say *please, please don't*, but she
wouldn't let the words up out of her stomach; because that was what he liked her
to say.

He was angry, and he was having fun,
and he was moving around the table.

She kept the table between them, moving back and sideways. She had the knife out in front of her, and its steel blade was sharp enough to do serious damage, pointing at his belly.

What if Tonnie was strong enough to take the knife — ?

She couldn't stand to think that. She wouldn't let herself think that.

"It's her father, she thinks if she can get people talking about me, he'll have to pay attention to her." Tonnie stopped moving now. He spoke in a loud voice over his shoulder to her mother, but his eyes watched Tish. "She thinks she can use me to get her father to come and take her to live with him. And let her get away with whatever she wants to, that's what she thinks."

"She knows better than that," Mom said.

Tish knew her father didn't want her living with him. She knew her father was glad when Tonnie adopted her legally, and took her off his hands. She had no dreams about her father.

She didn't even *want* to live with her father.

She didn't even know where he lived.

"Stupid," she called Tonnie, right to his face.

Without thinking.

And then Tonnie lost it. He lost it entirely and he roared, like a bull or a wild tiger. He picked up one end of the table and lifted it, dumping everything on it towards her — juice glasses, toast plate, salt and pepper, dirty napkins, half-full cereal bowls, spoons, bottle of candy vitamins for the kids, all crashed down onto the floor.

Tish jumped back.

The clatter and clash and smash and breaking of china and glass filled the room, and then stopped. In the silence, the TV talked on.

Tonnie set the table down, with a smile. "I'd better get to work now. I'll finish with you tonight. Tish."

She raised the knife.

"Let me remind you about a couple of things," Tonnie said, staring right at her while his fingers unbuttoned the wet shirt. "Barbie, get me another shirt, will you?" he called. "And undershirt, too. But, *not*" — calling after Tish's mother as she went down the hall — "a good shirt, don't get careless, I don't have the time to pick up after your messes this morning. Since I've wasted so much time on this particular mess," he called. He smiled at Tish.

He took his shirt off and hung it over the

back of a chair. She made herself not look away scared. He lifted his undershirt up over his head and dropped it onto the floor. She could stick the knife between the ribs, there, where the pulse was beating, and pull it sideways. If he started for her. Once she had the knife in, she could use both hands for pulling it sideways.

"Let me warn you about slander. Tish," his tongue seemed to own her name. "Because if you start telling this story around. You don't know anything about slander laws."

He was right, she didn't.

"Nobody'll believe you, anyway. Who'd believe you? You spend your time getting in trouble at school, who can say whether you're doing drugs or not, I wouldn't like to bet that you weren't, I couldn't swear to anything about you and most of us have a pretty good idea what you and that wimp Kipper get up to — so if you start this kind of scandal about me, I tell you, you'll be in a foster home so fast, your little butt will be smoking."

He smiled.

"Or," he corrected himself, "should I say your not-so-little butt?"

Everyone would believe his lies and not her truth.

That was true. Grownups believed grownups more than kids. She couldn't do anything to stop Tonnie doing whatever he wanted.

"Which — not-so-little butt — I plan to deal with tonight," Tonnie said.

"You stay away — " she said, but whispering like him. Her throat seemed to close, then open, and beat in soundless cryings like a fish flipped from its bowl out onto the floor. Her throat was too ashamed to let the words out. Her mouth wouldn't touch the words she said, or the words she wanted to say.

Why shouldn't her mother hear? — a voice screamed that in her head and

SHUT UP! she screamed right back.

"Did you ever hear of felonious assault?" he asked. Before she could say anything, he said, "For which crime people are sent to jail? What do you think the courts will do with a girl who turns against the man who adopted her with a knife? And raised her from the age of one year old? When her biologic father abandoned her? I'm not afraid of that silly knife," he said.

He meant it, and Tish could have wept then. Because if he wasn't afraid, then she'd better be.

"Felonious assault," Tonnie said again,

and he liked that idea so much that he went to meet Tish's mother, where she hurried down the stairs, and he let his wife help him get dressed — passing him the undershirt first, then holding out the long-sleeved shirt so he could slip his arms in easily, and helping him button it. Tonnie kissed his wife a long kiss good-bye, and Tish knew it was with his tongue, too, he made sure she could tell that. He opened his eyes and looked at her to be sure she was noticing all of this, before he let go of his wife and went out the door.

—Two—

If she'd been alone, Tish would have stayed still as glass. Until her arms stopped shaking. If she'd been alone she could have curled up on the floor, with her forehead against the cool linoleum, until her legs got strong enough to hold her upright again. If she'd been alone, Tish could have slipped down on to the floor and then gotten away from that body, and gone joyriding really alone, without that body touching her.

But she wasn't alone.

Her mother was right there, holding on to her elbows as if she were cradling something. Her mother's cheeks were pink and her eyes were wide, and her lips looked pillowy soft.

Tish had seen that look on people often enough to recognize it. She'd even almost felt that way herself, once or twice, unexpectedly, with Kipper. With Kipper, those unexpected times, there was something about —

If somebody put his arms around you to hold you close against his chest, and gentle, and you could hear his heart beating sometimes if you had your ear against his chest. It was safe when you were in his arms, and when he sometimes lifted your chin to kiss you, with his lips soft against your lips — The feeling took you by surprise, and was gone as soon as you recognized it — *Safe.*

Tish knew the look, she could almost imagine the feeling.

She just had trouble understanding how Tonnie could give her mom those feelings.

And that was a lie. Because sometimes — Because sometimes Tish was so dumb, she still hoped — As if, if someone would just love her, then she would stop caring about anything else — Because she did lie. The whole house was built on lies —

Like in Mexico City, built on a mud lake, and when that earthquake — buildings swallowed up into the mud, she couldn't help imagining about it — people stepping off seventeenth-floor balconies onto the ground, but nobody said anything about what about the sixteen floors underneath, no they'd skip thirteen because that was bad luck, only fifteen floors buried alive in —

That was what this house felt like. Tonnie's house that he owned.

Tish thought, if she lived in Mexico City, she would almost hope it would happen again, so she wouldn't have to be afraid of when it would happen again.

Or what Tonnie's feelings were, either. If Tonnie *had* feelings. Those she didn't understand at all, she couldn't imagine them and she didn't want to even think —

"Mom?" The sound of her own voice made her feel attached to herself again. Because she recognized her own voice, and she was so relieved that it was still there —

"Hmmnnh?" Her mother barely heard her. "What?"

That's what was all Tish could think of to say. Then she thought of something. "Want me to pick up this mess?"

"That would be nice, sweetie. I'll just finish . . ." Her mother drifted back to the kitchen sink, turned on the water, turned it off, turned around, one wet hand caressing her own cheek, as if trying to remember how a touch felt.

Tish could imagine that feeling, too.

It wasn't just bad memories she had, of her life. It wasn't just bad feelings. Even about Tonnie.

WRONG. She screamed it at herself, NOT TRUE, and it wasn't true, either. It just —

Her feelings were so strong, she couldn't even see them to name them. And they never stayed still, as if they were wild animals running around inside her. She hated most of them, and they knew it. She'd like to kill them, and that scared them, and it scared her, too, Tish thought. If that was any consolation.

Sometimes she didn't dare to think. Didn't dare to even start thinking.

She felt sorry for her mother, too, and she'd wanted Tonnie just for herself, too, and she had to admit she'd been jealous of Luley at first — the new baby, but it could all be jealousy, how could she be sure? She lied to herself, sometimes, she knew that, she didn't always know when she was lying, she had to admit that —

Some kids, some girls, were really alone, and living homeless, on the streets, turning tricks, and her life wasn't *that* bad. Compared to some. Like, compared to Miranda.

"Can you sit down with me for a minute, Sweetie?" Mom said. "Have a cup of coffee."

Tish didn't like coffee.

"I'll get to that mess later, it's no problem. It's nothing much, no time at all, when I get through you'll never know it happened. But there's time before the bus, because we need to talk. About Tonnie."

Almost, Tish wished her mother did know so she didn't have to protect her.

Tish sat down at the table again. She dumped four spoons of sugar into the mug of coffee, then two more, bent down to pick up the milk carton, shook it to hear if there was any left, poured milk into the mug, stirred. Her mother couldn't possibly know. That was the one good thing — while things with Tonnie got worse and worse, it would always have been even worse to have her mother know —

Her face felt hot, as if she were flushed. She rubbed her palm roughly across her mouth, and cheeks, and then pushed both palms into her eyes. She didn't want her mother to know.

That about her daughter.

Tish stared into the muddy coffee, because she couldn't find her hands to pick up the mug with, even if she'd wanted to drink.

"It's just his way," her mom said. "You mustn't mind him, Sweetie. Sweetie?"

Tish looked up. Her mom sat across the bare table, in Tonnie's seat. Her mom's elbows rested on the table, and her chin rested on her folded hands. Her mom's hair shone soft and clean, like silk. There was a little happy smile on her mom's lips.

"He doesn't mean anything by it. Why — that man — he'd cut off one of his own fingers before he'd let anyone hurt you."

Her mother didn't have a clue.

"That's better," her mother said. "Sweetie," her mother said, "I want you to know I understand. I really do. I know that when Tonnie — says things, about your complexion, for instance, or your figure — I know that hurts your feelings."

"Doesn't bother me," Tish said. Her jaw was tired. But why should she be angry at her mother?

"But there's nothing wrong with your complexion that time won't cure," her mother said. "I believe that. I truly believe it. Or your figure, although that'll take attention. And work. But it's not as if you're *fat*, is it? Tonnie just — he doesn't know how easy it is to hurt a girl your age."

Tish choked into her coffee.

"Don't you get smart with me, Tish. Being smart-alecky — trying to look superior — your father had that same look, and look what he did to me. If Tonnie hadn't come along . . ." her mom said. "It's not easy for Tonnie, so many children, and the economy the way it is. Not even Tonnie has job security these days. It's not that anybody has said anything, it's just, he just — he's not having an easy time right now. So he can't always think about your feelings as much as you'd like him to," her mother said.

Tish supposed it was something, that her mother had no idea.

"But you have to know how much he loves you," her mother said. Explained.

Tish shrugged. Love wasn't what she'd call it. But what did *she* know? Maybe this was exactly what love was.

"He always did," her mother said.

And they wondered why the divorce rate was so high, if this was what love was.

"I always said, it was you he really fell in love with, not me."

Tish had heard that, too, too often, often enough. It always made her feel sick, as if it were true.

"You weren't afraid of anything, when you were little. You still aren't," her mother said. "That's the thing he loves best about you."

If love was the magician with the saw in his hand, maybe she'd believe it.

"Why, I'd never dare pick a fight with Tonnie the way you did, with a knife, asking for trouble. . . . I've always known I need people to take care of me, but you've always been able to look out for yourself."

Ha, ha.

"I've never been good at looking out for myself," her mom said, smiling as she touched her swelling belly, as if she had a little warm secret tucked in there along with the baby.

"Tonnie saved our lives," Mom said.

So she had been told.

"Because I was at my wits' end. Literally at wits' end. Your father gone — walked out on us, walked out on his own child, not even a year old, no support money, even if I could have found him to ask, and my heart broken — "

"But you only married him because you got pregnant," Tish said. "With me."

"Who said that? Where did you get an idea like that?"

"From you," Tish reminded her mother.

"Your father and I got married because we were in love. Anyone who tells you different is lying. But he wasn't faithful to me, Tish. He had other women, all along."

"You told me you were pregnant," Tish insisted.

Her mother sighed. "Don't you care how I felt with a husband who had other women? No, don't bother, I don't expect you to — I just hope when it happens to you, you remember how I couldn't ask you for sympathy."

"You did say," Tish insisted.

"Why would I? It isn't true. We were young and in love and foolish. I never said that, and it's a terrible thing for you to say, Tish. It's a terrible thing to say."

"When I was — five, I think. You did tell me. It was summer. It was raining that day, all day, summer rain."

"Why do you want to think something like that about your own mother?"

"You were wearing red shorts, with flowers."

"Even if it was true, why would I want to tell you something like that?"

Tish didn't know. She only knew what she remembered.

But what if she was remembering wrong?

"You were angry at me," Tish remembered. "And you got married in September, you told me that."

"Well, that at least is the truth."

"And my birthday's in March."

"And? And? Do you know what year we were married? Miss Know Everything?"

Tish was tired. She didn't know why she cared. She didn't know. She didn't care.

And if she had cared, that would have done a lot of good, wouldn't it? Ha, ha.

"You don't know anything," her mom said then. "You don't remember what it was like at all. I had two full-time jobs just to keep a roof over our heads and food for the two of us, baby-sitting for you . . . Tonnie was a godsend to me."

"How much *was* the rent?" Tish asked. "What kind of jobs were they? Because it's really *terrible* if two full-time jobs can't earn you enough. What did you do?" She'd never wondered about that before.

"You know what I mean," her mother said. "Don't smart-mouth me. You've taken up talking back, and I don't know when that started."

Tish didn't bother caring. When she concentrated on her mother, she just felt so sorry for the woman. Just — really sorry for her, because she didn't know anything and she lied to everybody else and to herself, too, about everything.

"So will you forget this business with the knife?" her mother asked.

Which was the point of this whole conversation. Maybe her mother wasn't so stupid after all.

Tish didn't know what to answer. If she said No, then what if her mother asked *Why?* If she promised, she'd have been made into what they told her she was, a liar.

And she wasn't a liar. Not the kind of liar they said.

But if she told the truth — and her mother asked why — and she told the truth —

Her mother would lose everything again.

"The way you're acting, with a knife, it's not sensible, is it?" her mother asked now. "You were always so sensible, Sweetie, you were the most sensible little girl . . . but a knife. A knife is the way someone out of control might act."

Tish shrugged.

"Like that girl — Randy? And they say these things happen over and over again, in a community, among young people at the same school. Once it starts, they say, once it happens once. Did you know her?"

Tish nodded.

"But she wasn't a friend of yours, was she? Don't I know all your friends? And I don't remember ever hearing her name."

Tish nodded. All what friends? All what names? She didn't know where her mother got some of her ideas.

"Because the paper said that girl was an outsider. That was why, they said, and her weight, too, I'd guess, although they wouldn't say that, would they? The paper said," her mom lowered her voice, *"preg-nant.* What was this Randy girl's complex-ion like?"

"Miranda," Tish finally protested. *Terri-ble,* but that went along with Miranda's mousy hair in the kind of curls you got from sleeping in rollers every night, trying to have the kind of curly hair other girls did, her little marble-hard eyes and an acrid odor to her, people couldn't stand to be near her. It didn't matter anymore, but it was terrible, all of her.

"What?" her mother asked. "What do you mean by that?"

"Her name was Miranda. She used to be — before they moved, she was in my class. Up to third grade. She was fun, good at sports, too, she was fun to be around, and pretty, too. She was — one of the popular girls in the class."

"Well, she outgrew *that.* Did you see that picture in the paper?" her mother asked. "I don't know why they had to put a picture in, when she looked like that. And doing that to her father, poor man, and her mother buried not even two months ago? And don't I remember that her mother had one of those long sicknesses, that the poor man had

41

to nurse her through? And now his daughter goes and gets pregnant?"

Tish didn't want to talk about Miranda.

Her mother wanted to. "I guess it wasn't any surprise she was pregnant. That kind of girl — always ends up pregnant, doesn't she? That girl was just out of control. The poor father."

Miranda's father drove her to school every morning and picked her up at the end of every school day. Every day he came early and waited in the white station wagon at the end of the walkway. Tish had watched the fat girl lumbering out the doors and down the sidewalk to where the car waited. Waddle, waddle — her buns rolling up against one another — like a girl going down the hallway to the electric chair every day.

It was terrible how horrible Miranda had become. Tish had her own guess about how Miranda got that way. She secretly thought that Miranda had it worse, and she was secretly relieved that somebody had it worse, and she turned away, ashamed, whenever she saw Miranda. So they couldn't even help each other.

If there was any help.

And now that wasn't even a choice Tish

could make anymore, since Miranda had hanged herself.

"What's that smirk for?" her mother demanded. "I don't understand teenagers at all, I don't — "

"Sorry," Tish said, and lowered her head so her hair would hide her face, until the desire to giggle sank back down again. Miranda hanging naked from the tree right by the sidewalk in front of her father's house —

It was so bad, nobody even made jokes about it.

— so that when it got light, everybody would see her there. And her father wouldn't dare ever again to look anyone in the eyes for fear of what they might be thinking, or what they might see when they looked at him.

Served him right, Tish thought, fierce.

But it served Miranda wrong. Looked at that way, everything served Miranda wrong and that thought killed the giggles. "She wasn't," Tish said, now when it was too late. "She didn't whore around, not like that" — Because Miranda *had*, they all knew it, but it wasn't — "It's not what you think," she told her mother. "You don't know everything."

"No," her mother agreed. There was sadness in her voice now. "You'd think, after everything I've been through, I'd at least understand more." She stared into the mug of coffee. "But I keep thinking about her poor father."

"Why do you feel so sorry for him?"

"You're getting so *hard*, you didn't used to be so *hard*, Tish, and selfish — "

"I mean, Mom, if somebody does something like that, like Miranda did, something *has* to be wrong. Seriously wrong. That isn't normal, not even for people killing themselves, the way she did it."

" — or without sympathy for people. No feelings."

"But nobody is even asking. Everybody just says, 'Poor him.' What about her? What about Miranda? She's the one who's dead. She's the one who hanged herself. Not him. Don't you care about her at all? Why, because she's a kid and kids don't matter?" She knew she should stop the words, but she couldn't find the shut-up muscles for her mouth.

"Take it easy." Tish's mom reached across to catch Tish's arm, and hold it down on the table with her hands.

"Slow down, everything's okay. You're getting all worked up about this, Sweetie.

It happens, these things happen. Calm down, now, you know you've always been overemotional, you get all worked up — see, now you're crying and it's been almost a week since she did it, why should you cry now? Is there something wrong, Sweetie? You know I'll do anything I can for you, to help, is there something I can do?"

Tish was tempted. She was honestly tempted. To say it —

Not the whole truth, but —

Just, *He comes into my room,* and let her mother guess the rest. Let her mother understand without Tish having to say it. *He comes into the bathroom, he comes into my bedroom.*

But she'd already said all of that. And all that happened was, her mother had been struck deaf while those words were in the air.

Because her mother knew.

Because the TV was on so her mother couldn't hear, didn't have to hear, not with the TV on, not even when Tish yelled —

Because her mother already knew and refused to know.

If Tish insisted on the truth, she'd lose her mother.

Because the truth would make Tish free, and her mother didn't want her to be free.

As if her mother were the other girl in the magician's box.

Tish thought she might raise her face and howl, and howl, until the sound of her voice broke the whole world up into pieces.

"I need help, Mom," she said, and it was a whisper. It was funny that even while she was screaming away inside her head, her voice was a little whispery thing.

"I'm sorry, Sweetie. We can't." Her mother shook her head, sad again. "You know what Tonnie says. You know he'd never — and the insurance doesn't cover it and we can't afford it, we told the specialist that last year, remember?"

Tish remembered.

"When she suggested therapy because of your grades. Remember? When you always used to have all A's and then last midyear's grades it was D's. And an F in gym. And that woman, the education expert the school sent you to — I can't for the life of me remember her name. But she said she recommended psychological testing, and then she said probably some therapy. Don't you remember?"

Tish remembered. Ms. DelCippio, she had yellow teeth from smoking. Tish remembered it all. There had been hope — hope rising like the sun, like the sun rising in her belly. They said — everybody said — just try to tell us what you want. We want to help you if you'd only tell us what you want, or need. "It would help me, Mom," Tish said. "He doesn't have to know, does he?"

"Are you asking me to lie to my husband, Tish?"

Hope fled, and hopelessness fell down on her like a mountain. That was about the way it had felt last year, too, leaving Ms. DelCippio's office the last time.

"And then your grades came right back up, so Tonnie was right, wasn't he? It wasn't anything we couldn't handle ourselves."

Tish lowered her eyelids, to hide the anger she thought must show like lightning in her eyes, flashing across her eyes, flashing out of her eyes. Because she had done it herself, and Tonnie had tried to take it away from her by saying he guessed that showed that he was right after all, wasn't he, a little less of the social life, a little more firmness from him, and she was back in line in no time, and nobody needed any shrinks after all, did they, never mind so-called experts. He'd taken care of her himself, Tonnie said. He said that and she hated him, because she had done it herself. She had done it for herself. She had made up her own mind that whatever else, she wasn't going to give up her grades because of Tonnie. She wasn't going to be forced to give up anything more than she absolutely had to. Certainly not her life, no matter how bad it got. Not to the shame. Not to him. "Tonnie," she said, almost choking on the word.

"You sound like you don't like him, Sweetie," her mother said. "Do you have any idea how you sound? Like someone who hates men. Is that where this knife business comes from? You'll have to give it to him, Sweetie, this isn't a fight you can win."

Tish shook her head. "But he — " The words choked her, she was so ashamed and sorry. "He comes — " And afraid.

Her mother rose up from the chair, to leave the table. "Stop it right now. Just stop it. You can't just go around spreading lies like that, Tish. You can't just spread lies."

Because her mother really did know.

Her mother knew, and didn't care.

"I don't," Tish muttered.

Her mother was going to call the boys for their bus. She turned around. *"What did you say?"*

"Don't lie!" Tish hollered. "I'm not! I never did!" She knew who the liars were.

"Well," her mother said, smiling at her

own sarcasm. "That's news to me. Remember the Veronica comic you said Angie gave you?"

"That was stealing," Tish said. "Not lying."

"Oh, I see now. I guess I wasn't thinking. And it wasn't lying when you told me Angie gave it to you?" her mother asked.

"That's different," Tish said. *Not fair,* she thought. I was six years old. If the only example you can think of is from when someone was six years old, it isn't *fair* to say she's a liar.

"Oh, is that so?" her mother asked.

Did her mother think Tish would never figure out the true situation? How could her mother think that?

"And do you think I don't know who keeps taking my birth control pills?" her mother asked.

Tish froze. If her mother was asking, at last, Tish wasn't about to lie, and she wasn't going to tell the truth, and she wasn't even going to ask her mother in that case why she had gone to different clinics and gotten three separate prescriptions for the pills, as if she thought she was supposed to go on taking the pills when she was pregnant, and had all those prescriptions filled so there were months and months of them in the medicine chest. . . . Who did her mother think she was fooling?

But her mother wasn't asking a question for Tish to answer it. Her mother was going down the hall like someone who just won the war for the right side, and Tish picked up her backpack from the hall table, and jammed the knife into it, and got out of the house.

—Three—

Tish walked to school. About a mile. It took about twenty minutes. The walk, not school. School took about six hours, but she could stretch it out to eight or sometimes nine. Tish could have taken the bus to school, and some days she did, but not usually. Usually she chose to walk.

Usually she took the extra time to walk, alone.

She needed the time alone to become whatever she was going to be on any particular day, since she made a point of not ever being the same as she had been the day before, as much as she could. Just like she made a point of not wearing anything like the same kind of clothes from one day to the next. So nobody could ever know what to expect of her. So nobody could ever think they knew her well enough to know her. She always looked different from the days before.

Unless it was one of the two or three times a year when she wore exactly the same outfit for days in a row.

Except underwear, of course. Tights, too, if it was an outfit with tights. But everything else she kept the same, exactly the same.

Tish was in charge of whatever anybody might think they knew about her. Being unpredictable was her usual MO, for safety. It looked like an MO for style, but Tish knew better.

One of the first things Tish did, once she had gotten out of the house in the morning, was fish around in her backpack and take out the big sweepstakes envelope she'd rescued from their trash, to replace the earlier sweepstakes envelope when it got too worn, which had itself replaced an even earlier sweepstakes envelope — they'd been running sweepstakes for years and years. She couldn't figure out why nobody ever seemed to know anybody who had won it, but people kept on entering, people were hopelessly greedy, or maybe they just didn't know how to know when they had no hope at all.

The pills were in a little envelope, the kind cheap kids' valentines got put into, inside the big envelope. Tish figured, nobody would even be curious about the big envelope, but if they were, the little envelope didn't give anything away, either. Except maybe that she was a dope who still carried around some grade-school valentine she'd gotten, maybe, unless carrying around an old grade-school valentine turned out to be a really cool thing to do. People could think what they wanted about whether or not Tish was a dope, or cool, or what. What people thought about that didn't matter. The pills mattered.

She fished a pill out and swallowed it, and almost at once it was like — being safe. As if the inside of her uterus had been lined with barbed wire and signs saying *No Babies Here*. The pills were ninety-eight percent effective. She walked along, counting — how long since her last period began, because with the pills periods were as regular as clockwork, she was pretty sure she was safe.

Ninety-eight percent sure.

Ninety-eight percent safe.

She moved the knife from the backpack to her boot.

On bad mornings, Tish had trouble finding her feet, to make them walk. On bad mornings, it was like her body was a puppet, and she had to make it work, but she almost couldn't figure out what string to pull to make her feet come off the ground, one after the other, pulling the string from inside her head, foot up, down forward, up, forward down.

Every day was a bad morning.

She concentrated, as she walked, on imagining it. As if she were an actress in the movies, pretending so hard, in her imagination, that she was actually doing it. Walking. Being the walking girl. As if she were the director, directing the actress about walking — "Relax, kid, don't make it such a big deal" — and how to carry her bookbag — "You look like some whipped dog, straighten *up*, kid" —

Randy must not have been on the pill, Tish thought, and how Randy could not have been on the pill, every month having to wait, and hope, and look at your underpants in fear —

"Get some expression into it, kid," the directing voice told her.

Yesterday — Tish tried to picture yesterday, tried to picture looking down at her yesterday self because she never went near mirrors — she wore a skirt yesterday, something with a skirt, flower print, a dress — she'd gotten it for a dollar at the Thrift Stores; no, she lied, it was a dollar twenty-nine. Yellow and green, yesterday. Yesterday was giggles and gum, and today was the survival knife. Today was a *Tough* day, a *Give Me Room* day.

"That's more like it," the director's voice told her.

Oh get lost, she told it, and it obeyed.

The knife was giving her trouble. She was carrying the knife tucked into her right-foot Doc, where she could get at the handle but nobody would see it, tucked inside the boot top. But it felt like everyone would see it. And know she had it. And wonder why she had to carry it.

Tish hesitated, standing still in her imagination, on one foot like a stork. And she almost panicked. She almost thought she had ruined everything with the survival knife.

But what was the big deal? Hey, maybe she was working on being a world-champion mumbly-peg player, what did anyone know about Tish, and who she was, anyway? Nobody knew anything, so nobody knew if anything was impossible. So if she had this knife, no big deal, she had a knife. Nobody's business.

Okay. Okay.

She was feeling okay. Ready to get through the day.

This was going to be a swagger day.

Last night was over. Gone. Flushed away into the past. Last night was history.

Tonight was the future, and there was always the chance that the future wouldn't ever arrive — Somebody might, for example, push the famous red button and finish off the world —

Tish wasn't sure how she felt about that. Part scared, sure. But only part relieved. Only part of her was relieved to have her life over with, nothing more that could be done to her. The remaining part was sorry — sorry she'd never get a chance.

Chance for what? What kind of a chance did she have, already, anyway? Sometimes Tish thought she really *was* so dumb, she really did deserve it. Thinking she had a chance for a life. The best she could hope for was that she'd get a chance to rip Tonnie's guts out tonight. Big chance. Great chance. Lucky Tish.

Anyway, tonight wasn't a problem yet, being a whole day away.

And she had the knife now. And he knew it, because she'd told him.

So tonight would be different. It had to be.

But different how?

Tish tried to forget the night coming, and concentrate on the day just ahead, on school. *It was a swagger day.* She swaggered on down the street. Trying not to think.

How if, instead of being frightened off, Tonnie treated it like a game, like when they'd play ping-pong if she was playing well, he came down on her like a ton of bricks and really creamed her, but if she played bad and weak, he just beat her and that was that.

A don't mess with me day.

If he took the survival knife for a challenge, not a threat. Made the threat into a dare.

An Oh, yeah? day.

And if she had to use the knife and cut him, and he called the police — felonious assault was one of his stupid sound-smart phrases, but still, when you went after somebody with a knife, even if it was self-defense, you ended up in court. She thought. On TV you did, she was pretty sure. Or what if she got lucky and killed him?

An instant lifting of the heart, she thought

she remembered the feeling, gladness, an instant of — heart, gladness — was that some memory? When — ?

An instant of imagining Tonnie dead before awareness of her own ignorance rode in on the wave of fear that crashed over her head. She didn't know anything about what was self-defense in legal cases.

And she couldn't break down. Not here. Not on her way to school.

Tish forgot. As best she could. She swaggered on down the street. Forgetting last night. Forgetting the night that was coming.

If she could forget right away, before any memory got inside her skin, then she'd make it through the day okay. If any memories got in — like acid, they burned her, and she was trapped in her skin with them, burning into her skin, burning out through it, burning in to find her stomach and burn her out.

Because she wasn't sure how long she'd be able to go on hiding in her skin. She wasn't sure she was hidden far enough away inside, so nobody could figure it out. Because if anybody figured it out —

She almost could not *walk*, just thinking about that —

Even to think of it, it was as if acid ate at her belly, because if kids *knew*, if people at school knew and looked at her —

She'd rather die. It was that simple. She'd rather be dead and done with than have anyone know what really happened in her life, and how they'd look at her like dirt. Like dirt they felt sorry for. Like having to go naked and ugly to school — without a shower, and your teeth never brushed, no comb, naked and ugly and un-taken care of —

All the secret, private parts exposed, and all the stuff that didn't show from under clothes, and the hairy parts unhidden, and everybody looking at you — naked — everybody seeing you —

While everybody else had all their clothes on.

If that were to happen —

She'd —

Just thinking of it, her heart shriveled up in her, and her stomach shriveled up in her, and she shriveled up inside her skin. Outside she was swaggering down the street, her Docs clumping on the pavement like jack-boots, her shoulders back and swinging.

But, inside —

Inside she was a mess —

Inside she was shriveled up like that skeleton at the start of *Star Wars*, burned down to only hunched bones face down on the ground, like what was left of a person after all the horrible things anyone could think of to do to him had been done.

Inside, shame rose up, and she couldn't swallow fast enough to keep it down —

And there was the danger that anyone looking at her eyes could see the truth of her.

Her whole body came to a halt, like a dry leaf flamed in the fire. She twisted in her shame, and turned — except her feet were heavy, pulling her down into a drowning of shame —

A deep breath. Another. And she shuddered.

The black toes of her Docs, and the heavy laces, when she looked at them, caught her attention. They were kickers, those boots. They had the weight and heft and stiffness of sole for kicking, and she had the legs to use them, and a knife, too —

Three deep breaths. Four.

She combed fingers through her hair. Lipstick, bright red lipstick, that was what she needed. As soon as she got to school, even before she found Kipper to say Hey to, she'd get Angie to give her some bright red lipstick. And she'd paint her mouth with it, and then who *knew* what she'd say? With that mouth, she could say anything, the wilder the better.

And she had the knife, and she'd use it on him, if she had to, no matter what about after.

The Docs ate up the pavement. Tish didn't want to be late to homeroom. She didn't want to draw anybody's fire. The strength in her legs reassured her, and the lift of her feet taking her along to school, and the thought of how the red lipstick would look — a slash of bright color. *Don't mess with me.*

Four

She had time for only a quick hello to Kipper, and a brief kiss, before the home-room bell.

Kipper was cool with that. A brief kiss was about all he wanted from her. His last girlfriend had expected a lot of him, by way of attention, like phone calls and movies and taking her to parties and dances, as well as some pretty heavy-duty physical stuff. His last girlfriend had pretty much taken over his life, or anyway, that was Tish's impression of how things had been. So Kipper was cool with whatever limits Tish set on things. "You're so easy to be with," he kept saying. Usually, he said that when they weren't going to see each other, except in school, for a while. Easy to be with meant Tish didn't take much of his time. Easy to be with, in Kipper's book, was really good.

"You, too," she'd answer and he'd say, "What do you know? I'm the first guy you ever went with."

"Yeah, sigh, sigh, my first boyfriend," she'd say, sarcastic, her hands clasped together at her heart. "My practice boyfriend," she'd say. And that was the truth, to see if she could have a boyfriend without giving away what she was really like. She was supposed to be inexperienced — and she was, too, just not the way she was supposed to be — so all the feelings she did wrong would have a reason. If she was inexperienced, she was bound to be a little weird about a boyfriend, and not know how to have one. Kipper wanted a girlfriend who would leave him be. A girlfriend who didn't want a real boyfriend. And Tish felt the same, only vice-versa.

They suited each other, she and Kipper. Both of them brief kissers.

Tish slipped through the door to homeroom and slid into her desk too late to join in any talk, but in time for roll call. "Here," she answered to her name, not even really listening, just sitting behind a pile of books until the bell rang. She hadn't cut her hair for a while. Maybe she'd do that tomorrow, maybe hack her hair really short at the front. Let Tonnie have a good look at her zits.

She drove Tonnie out of her head.

He'd keep coming back, she knew, all day, and she'd keep driving him away, all day. She knew that. There were some good things she knew about herself, like, she could stand there at the inner edge of herself driving Tonnie out of her head all day long, and keep on doing it. Because if she didn't —

And like, it took only seven years for every cell in your body to be replaced, so in seven years from this morning she would be completely new, a completely new person.

The bell rang.

Tiffany stopped her in the hallway. "You look *great*, Tish, sort of — French, that's it, like some actress from a French movie."

"Groovy," Tish said. "Or should I say *magnifique*?" She sounded like some actress, too, the voice she heard herself speaking in.

"You've got such a great sense of style," Tiffany said. "I wish I had your sense of style."

"*Moi aussi,*" Tish laughed, walking away. Tiffany was too dim a bulb to notice the insult. If she did, Tish would deny it. "I

64

said," she could hear her own voice answering Tiffany's whiny one, *"we'll see.
Did you misunderstand? I'm sorry, Tiff. I
meant to be hinting that maybe you do
have a sense of style, but it'll come out
more when you're older."* "D'you mean
that?" the imagined Tiffany asked, pleased
and humble. "Sure," the imagined Tish
lied.

Whatever she was being on any given
day, at school, with the people who might
think they were her friends, Tish had to pretend a couple of things consistently. She had
to pretend she didn't care what anybody
thought of her, and she had to pretend that
non-caring was an act, and she was secretly
a nice person. Or else —

Mrs. Wyse kept the same motto on the
board for days. "The truth shall set you
free." The first time Tish had seen that, she'd
— She didn't know *what* she'd do, for a
minute, and she was scared, because — If
she started bawling, for instance, or went
up to the board and just underlined every
word of it, and put in exclamation points
after every word. The first time Tish had
seen that motto on Mrs. Wyse's board was
the second day after Miranda had offed
herself.

Tish sat down at her desk and looked at those words waiting for her on the board, just words in a line, and she felt her heart tremble.

Mrs. Wyse started off the class by saying it was a week since Miranda's death. Every other teacher was ignoring Miranda, and what she'd done, or maybe they'd forgotten by now, and the kids tried to forget her, although it would kind of pop up in conversations, like fat-flesh through tights with holes in them. One person would push the subject down, and it would pop out of somebody else's mouth.

Not in Mrs. Wyse's class, however. Not Mrs. Wyse. Mrs. Wyse wasn't afraid of anything anyone might say or think. "It's been a week," she said. "Since Miranda was found dead. It's only been a week. Or you could say it's already been a week. Today, I'd like to ask for a minute's silence, in her memory."

Silence entered the room, swelling to fill it, like flood waters rising, or a flower opening out its petals. Tish studied her hands and thought of Miranda. Poor Miranda. "Sorry," she thought, "sorry," as if something were her fault. Then she wondered why Mrs. Wyse had said "was found dead" and not "died" — as if Miranda had died first and then hanged herself? And she probably had, Tish thought. Died over and over. Until the hanging must have felt like such a big relief, it could feel like your own birthday party, hanging yourself at the end of a rope off a tree in your front yard, until you died.

The whole room was as quiet as a test. Quieter. Somebody snuffled — Megan, Tish saw, raising her head, and Chrissie was digging into her backpack to find a tissue and pass it to Megan, or maybe to blow her own nose, and Mrs. Wyse said in her normal teacher voice, "Yes, thank you. Now, today. . . ."

Tish opened a notebook, waited.

"How about thinking by opposites today? What would that be in this case? Jerry? What's the opposite of *The truth shall set you free?* Any ideas?"

"Truth'll get you sent to jail?"

"If you're Ollie North."

Ideas went bouncing around the room like bouncing balloons. Some full of hot air, some empty — bounce, bounce. Tish doodled in her notebook.

"Or if you get date-raped by Willie Smith."

"She didn't go to jail, did she? That would be really terrible."

"Neither did he. It was Tyson who went to jail."

"Yeah, and guess what color he is."

"Is a better opposite something like, *Lies shall set you free?*"

"Deep, man, that's deep."

In Tish's notebook the page was filling up with boxes in boxes in boxes, like some maze.

"Lies *will* set you free, not shall." Mrs. Wyse stuck in a little grammar.

"Then *truth shall* is wrong, too, isn't it, Mrs. Wyse?"

"Yes, good. It's archaic, that's why it's all right. It's idiomatic usage, otherwise you're right, it's wrong."

"But will lies set you free? Do you think that? Is lying better for us than telling the truth? Is that what you want us to think?"

"I just want you *to* think," Mrs. Wyse said. "There's nothing in particular *that* I want you to think." She hesitated. "Except, maybe, clearly. Or," she added, grinning away at her own joke, "if clearly isn't possible, with the intention to be honest. What part of speech are those modifiers? Danielle?"

"I was raising my hand to say something else."

"That's okay, but do you know what part of speech *clearly* is?"

"Heather would, but she's absent," Danielle said. "Oh," she put her hand over her mouth. "Oops."

Tish knew what *clearly* was, in grammar, and about Heather, too.

Somebody offered an excuse. "There's sickness in Heather's family, like a grandparent, I think I heard it was a grandparent, and they all went for a visit. Or maybe an aunt? Really sick. If they might die."

Tish thought she knew better. Not that anyone had told her anything, but she'd seen Heather and Angie in close conference, and Heather was looking pale, and weepy, and for days Steve had been avoiding Heather, who'd gone around asking where he was; and now Chrissie was very carefully not giving anything away in her expression. Chrissie's face was like a mask, with only the eyes real, and the eyes didn't give anything away. Whenever anything was going on, Chrissie always knew. Tish almost never did — she didn't hear about any secrets until everyone knew them.

Tish didn't have anything like a best friend. She was an odds-out person, who didn't belong anywhere but almost fit in with most people —

Which was the way she wanted it. She didn't know what she'd do if she had a close friend, who expected to know all about her. Angie knew about Heather, you could tell by the way secrets lifted up the ends of Angie's little smile, and danced in the corners of her eyes, peeping out, hoping to be seen and get attention. Tish could make a good guess about which of Heather's relatives was sick, and sick with what, and how they were curing it.

If Heather had told the truth, Tish wondered now, would she be free? Wasn't Heather already choosing freely? But she had to figure Heather was ashamed, since it was being kept such a secret.

Or somebody was ashamed.

And if Miranda had told the truth, if Tish's guess was right, what would have happened then? Who would be free now? Or would it make no difference at all.

"Lies are the jail," Jason said.

"Deep, man."

Jason refused to back down. "Well, they are."

"More like shackles than jail," Larry suggested. "You know? Those ankle cuff things? With chains connecting your ankles? And you can't move around in them?"

"What do the rest of you think of that?"

Mrs. Wyse asked. "Do you feel like —
what? — like there are lies that hold you
back and slow you down and trip you up
and — what? — will pull you down and
drown you with their weight?"

Tish could almost taste that black water.
She almost couldn't breathe.

"Death sets you free," she called out, calling it out over the other voices.

"Not so loud, Tish," Mrs. Wyse said, but
she was interested.

"Deep, man."

"Groovy."

Tish was sorry she hadn't kept her big
mouth shut.

"That's so cynical, Tish. Even for you, it's
so — cynical."

Tish smiled, because if she hadn't smiled
she didn't know what she might have done
with her mouth.

"Lies do do that, though," Chrissie said.
"Like, I know when I lie — "

"Come off it, Chrissie."

"You expect us to believe that Miss Perfect
tells lies?"

"Yes, I expect you to believe it. Just because *you've* decided I'm perfect doesn't
mean I am. And I'll tell you something else.
I like getting away with lies. You know?"

They knew.

"But it also drags me *down*."

Tish knew that dragged-down drowning.

She was surprised that Chrissie did, too, but if Tish knew one single thing for sure, it was that people weren't what it looked like they were, so she was never surprised by people. But she wondered what Chrissie's lies looked like. Tish's own lies —

"I broke into the neighbor's house," Tish said, lying loudly. "They were away on vacation, they'd taken a driving vacation to the Grand Canyon. And the Alamo, too, because their little boy said he didn't want to go anywhere with them unless he got to see where Davy Crockett died. He was only seven, but pretty much of a full-grown monster," she said.

She had no idea where this would end up.

"He sounds like my little sister."

"He sounds like my little brother."

"I used to baby-sit him," Tish said. "He'd never go to bed until he got me to give him special treats. Like TV programs, and food. It was like, more TV, more food, every time, or he wouldn't go to bed. A monster."

"He sounds like *me*," Danielle giggled.

Tish grinned at her, a big false grin.

"When you broke into the house, what'd you do?" Tiffany asked, and a few people said only Tiffany would actually believe this, but Tish answered her question anyway. As long as Tish acted like she thought she was telling a true story, nobody could say for sure it wasn't true, as long as nobody cared enough to check it out. As long as the story she was telling was interesting enough so people could wish it were true, enough to pretend they believed her.

"Not much." Tish pictured the scene, as if she were watching a movie, wondering what she would see happening next. "Watched an X-rated movie the father had hidden in a drawer."

"Cool. Tell us about it."

"Yeah. Blow by blow."

Tish shook her head, grinning away. "You're not old enough."

"Yeah, yeah. Like we really believe this."

"I ate ice cream and potato chips."

"Gee whiz, Tish, how did you get so bad?" Sarcastic. But sarcasm was normal, and that was good, someone being sarcastic at her. That meant she was getting away with looking normal.

"I wrote stuff on the mirrors, in her lipstick."

"What kind of stuff?"

Tish shrugged. "Just what you'd expect. Just — you know."

They guessed they did.

"The cops asked everyone in the neighborhood, all the kids, if they knew anything. And their parents. My stepfather almost got into a fight with one of the cops, because the guy didn't believe me. It was sort of fun. Sort of like having a gun, or a knife hidden in your boot when everyone thinks you're helpless."

They were all listening.

"So I had to give myself up because otherwise my stepfather might have gotten himself into serious trouble."

"Then what happened?"

"Oh — " Tish spread her hands out on the desk and let shame hunch her shoulders forward, because she didn't have to pretend when it came to shame. And the memory of fear. She mumbled, "I had to go over there, and tell them myself, and apologize and then my stepfather got after me pretty bad with his belt."

"Wait a minute. He wears one of those Navajo belts, doesn't he? Those mothers are heavy."

"Naw, he'd never use that one on her. It'd get blood all over it," Jerry said, and they laughed. They didn't believe a word of what she said. They believed Tish was lying about lying.

Tish shrugged at her audience, let them believe what they wanted to, and now that she'd made up that whole long stupid story, she thought about the question. Now that there was no danger, she would open her mouth and tell the truth.

"Because it's degrading to have to lie," Tish said.

That was it, exactly, and she said the word again because it was so perfect.

"Degrading."

Then everyone was quiet, until Mrs. Wyse asked, "Anyone else have anything to contribute on this subject? No? Okay, then, let's talk about adverbial clauses."

"Wait," Andy said, "I've got something to say."

"Too late," Mrs. Wyse said.

"No, it's important. It's smart. You'll like it."

"Tomorrow," Mrs. Wyse said.

It flashed across Tish's mind: What waited between *now* and *tomorrow*. Would the knife make a difference? Would it make all that much difference? Because if it didn't, *tomorrow* tasted like ashes in her mouth, like blood and ashes and salt tears, and her stomach burned.

And she was sitting on the window sill, looking out, looking at the way clouds lay across the sky with their wrinkles and ridges and soft, puffy pillowiness. She was sitting curled up on the window sill looking out, holding on to the thread that connected her to Tish who was sitting at her desk, doodling boxes in her notebook. She held the thread tight in her hand so she didn't get completely lost.

Lunch wasn't possible. Tish picked out the soup, and a box of milk, and ice cream to put on her spoon and not-eat in little nibbling bites. She sat with the usual — Chrissie, Angie, Danielle, Shantal, Jen and Judy, Megan, Maria, Tiffany. Lindsay and Crystal were absent that day, too, along with Heather, but Tish didn't know why about them. The usual bunch of them had their usual end section of a long cafeteria table, and sat down in no particular order. Some days they all talked together, some days they broke up into separate conversations. They weren't really a clique, although sometimes it looked like they were. That day, Angie looked up at Tish to say, "Does it bother you? Or not, the way Mrs. Wyse keeps bringing up Randy."

Tish shrugged. She set her tray down at the end of the table. Without a word, they slid along to make room for her, led by

Chrissie, who was at the other end of the line of girls. Tish didn't bother thanking anyone. She straddled the table leg, at the end of the bench. She was in Don't Mess With Me mode. She was in Catch Me If You Can mode.

"You guys think Mrs. Wyse knows?" Jen asked, looking hopefully around.

"Knows what?"

"About Heather? And Steve, you mean?"

"Everybody knew about Heather and Steve, she practically took out an ad in the paper when he gave her his letter sweater. How could anyone not know?"

"They don't, sometimes. Teachers, parents. They're pretty dumb sometimes. Adults," Shantal said. "They don't think we have real lives."

Megan added, "As if they've forgotten — I mean, they *have* to have been our age, right? At some point. To get to their age."

Maria said, "They want us to be different from them. Innocent. Children carry the burden of innocence for adults."

"Look out, world — there goes Maria up into the stratosphere."

"Like sin eaters," Maria explained, paying no attention to the mockery.

Tish remembered those sin eaters. They had to eat the food that carried all the sins a dead person had committed in his life, so the dead person could get into heaven. Or her life, her sins.

"And they despise us for being powerless. Which is actually just an aspect of innocence," Maria continued. "And they're jealous of us, too."

Tish knew about exactly how those sin eaters felt.

She took the spoon out of her soup. She never liked noodle soup, anyway. Maybe the ice cream would go down okay.

"I think innocence is a real turn-on for some people," Maria said. "If you ask my opinion."

"Which — frankly — I didn't," Angie complained. "You're getting so cynical — you sound almost as bad as Tish."

Which she wouldn't have been able to say, if she'd thought Tish really was all that bad. Or, if she'd known how bad, in reality. So Tish could blow the paper wrapper of her straw across at Angie's face, and it could be a joke. "Put a lid on it, Angie," Tish said.

Ha, ha.

"Well, *I* think Mrs. Wyse knows, and I think," Danielle burst into speech, "Heather told her. I saw them talking after school, in the classroom, and Heather was crying."

"In front of Mrs. Wyse? At school?"

Tiffany asked. She covered her face with her hands in sympathy for the shame. "Creepy."

"Well, how can you blame Heather for crying? From what I heard. What I heard was that Steve told her he didn't even believe it was his baby," Jen smirked around at all of them. Her voice slid underneath the cafeteria sounds. Nobody but the people right near her could have heard what she said. "Can you believe it?"

"Do you think Mrs. Wyse advised Heather to get an abortion?"

"I couldn't do that, ever. I'd rather have the baby and have it adopted."

"Yeah? And where would you live, while you were waiting? With your mom and her boyfriend? They'd love that . . . *NOT*," Judy blared the last word. "And who'd pay to take care of you while you were being pregnant?"

"I hope Heather's okay. She probably is, isn't she?" Megan asked. "It's a statistically safe operation, under present conditions."

"If Mrs. Wyse advised her to get an abortion, she could be in trouble," Chrissie said, "so probably she didn't. If she did, she could be sued, or the school could."

They all got it. Chrissie's father was a lawyer, and Chrissie looked at things like a lawyer might, and knew stuff none of the rest of them did. They got the hint.

"Anyway," Jen said, "I wasn't talking about Heather, I was talking about Randy. About what it said in the paper. About her being pregnant."

"How do they know?" Tiffany asked.

"An autopsy," Maria said.

"Ugh."

"I don't want to even think about it."

"How pregnant, did they say?" Megan asked.

"Six months." It made Judy angry.

"Wow. That's really pregnant."

They were all thinking, what was going on six months ago.

"Being pregnant makes it even worse, don't you think?" Chrissie asked, but not talking to any one person.

"Why should they put something like that in the paper?" Judy demanded. "It doesn't make any difference now."

"What I heard," Tiffany said, "was that she was going after every boy in the school, like, for a couple of months." She giggled, her cheeks turned pink, and Tish knew what Tiffany was thinking, and was about to say, and she couldn't think of any way to stop the talking. "They all said. She was . . . she'd come up to them . . . asking, you know?

. . .'' She giggled, covered her face with her hands, and finished, "You know."

From where she was floating just under the ceiling, Tish could see the tops of all of their heads. Even her own, and she could watch her own hand move the spoon from the ice cream to her own mouth, and then put it back, and see how nobody noticed that no food was going in.

From overhead you could see how dark Tiffany's roots were, and the curls springing up from Maria's scalp, and the painted design on the barrette that held Chrissie's hair off her face.

From overhead, Tish could see how stiff she must look, if anyone looked, and scared, and in trouble. Tish was about to be in trouble and she better do something about it, she told herself.

"Boys," Judy said, disgusted.

"But *Randy*," Angie protested. "She was — gross. I know it's mean to say, but it's true. She wasn't even sexy."

Tish made herself swallow some ice cream and feel it cold in her throat, because if anyone noticed her faking it, they might ask questions.

"How *could* they?" Jen whispered, as if she was embarrassed to ask. "The boys. Especially if she was pregnant."

"Kipper says she didn't," Tish said, and that was the truth.

"Because she gave guys what they want," Judy explained to Jen.

"Pu-lease," Tiffany said. "Not while I'm eating."

Tish's stomach churned in shame.

"And yesterday, you know, I heard she had AIDS," Shantal said.

"No, it was crabs and that's not serious."

"I thought it was syph."

"Kipper told me." Tish made herself make them hear what she had to say. "If you didn't want to, she'd leave you alone." It was the most she could do for Miranda. It stopped them for a minute.

"Every boy I talked to yesterday was scared enough. That's for sure."

"But they all use rubbers," Tish said.

"What? What? Tish, how do *you* know that?"

"Kipper says. Because you'd be a real jerk off not to, he says."

"I don't *believe* what you two talk about," Tiffany said.

Tish shrugged.

"I wish I could find a boyfriend who'd talk to me like that, like I was a real person," Chrissie said, and then she said, "My father says you should always get your facts clear.

What's true can be pretty tricky, he says, but facts you can pin down."

Chrissie's mother had gone off when Chrissie — the oldest of three children — was ten, leaving Chrissie's father a single parent. He'd had a couple of long-term girl-friends since, and the present one Chrissie said she wouldn't mind if he married. That's what Chrissie claimed, but Tish didn't know if she believed it. Chrissie probably couldn't be as nice as she acted; it didn't make sense that anyone could be that nice.

But every now and then Chrissie would fix you with a look, or say something — and Tish was afraid of how smart Chrissie was. You weren't supposed to be so nice, and smart, too; that was a dangerous combination.

"We know for a fact that Randy's dead," Jen said. And laughed.

"Her name was Miranda," Tish told them all.

"That's not the kind of fact we mean," Jen told Tish. "Another fact is that she slept around."

"And around, and around," Angie giggled.

"Do we?" Tish demanded. Just to make trouble, but if she had to sit there, she thought she'd just as soon make a little trouble. Somebody should make a little trouble for Miranda, she thought. "Do we actually know anything, or have we just been told? Told by boys who want to make you think they're such big shots, too. Do we know it for an actual fact?"

"I never *watched*, if that's what you mean."

"No, I mean do we have any proof?" Tish insisted.

"You're pretty sick, Tish. What do you think would make proof? Everybody knows, isn't that proof enough?"

"Everybody knows squat," Tish said, and there was anger and disgust in her voice that surprised her. She shut herself up.

Chrissie was fixing her with one of those looks. Tish leaned her cheek on a hand and stared right back, being a blank wall.

"What about your famous Kipper?"

"He told her no."

"You believe everything Kipper says?"

Tish thought about it. "Yeah."

"No, but listen," Chrissie said. "It's a real question. Did anyone — no, be serious, Angie, I think Tish is making sense. Because Kipper doesn't have the kind of hang-ups most guys have — did any one of us ever talk to someone who actually slept with her? Or, is it they were always talking about what someone else did?''

Nobody could answer her.

The silence grew.

Tish was sorry she'd started it. She should have stayed shut up. Because if people started thinking —

"If she was pregnant," Maria said, "then there was a father. What about the father?"

Danielle finished her carton of milk and put it down neatly into the corner of the tray. "Okay, it's a fact that Randy was naked, which is pretty weird. So maybe that means something."

Tish was busy holding on to the edges of her tray, so she couldn't be bothered to repeat Miranda's name. She had to hold on, or she'd fly off, away, and they'd catch her at it.

"And she had that suitcase, packed. Set down beside the tree."

"Why would she have packed a suitcase?"

"Do you think she was murdered?"

"Do you think maybe the baby's father murdered her and made it look like suicide so he wouldn't have to marry her?"

"But nobody could make him. All he'd have to do is pay child support," Chrissie pointed out, "and that's practically impossible to collect if the father wants to avoid paying it. Although he might not have been aware of that."

"But six months pregnant is serious."

"And nobody *said* anything," Jen said. "I never heard anything about anything like this. Did anyone else?"

Nobody had.

"She could have had an abortion."

"Unless she didn't have any money. Unless she didn't have anyone to ask for help."

"Unless she was pretending it wasn't true, as long as she could," Chrissie suggested.

Tish swallowed.

"Who do you think the father was?"

"It could be anyone."

"Unless she was raped. What if — ?"

"You didn't have to rape Randy. That's the point. It would never be rape," Tiffany said.

"Wrong." Judy slammed her fist down on the table, every time she said the word: "Wrong. Wrong. Wrong. Rape is when the woman doesn't want to. No matter what else — no matter *what* — if the woman says no, the guy *has* to listen to her. Or else it's rape." She looked at them all, as if anyone dared to argue with her. "End of subject."

"Or if the guy says no," Tish said. What

right did Judy have to be so sure? What did Judy know about anything?

"Never mind that," Megan said, "what if? Never mind the rape question, what about Randy?"

"She'd have told." Shantal seemed pretty sure. "For the attention, if for no other reason, and also because the important thing is that guys don't just get away with it. Everybody knows that now."

"Do you really think she'd have told?" Danielle asked. "I'm not sure I would. I'm not sure I'd want to — get all that started."

"I'd be too embarrassed," Tiffany said.

"I wouldn't," Tish said.

"But you're so strong, and you don't care, you're not afraid of anything. Or anyone. What you wouldn't let people get away with doesn't count, Tish."

"Although Kipper makes me wonder about you. I mean, he's cute — really cute in a sixties way, I guess — but he's not exactly — a stud."

"It's easy to underestimate Kipper," Chrissie said. "Isn't that right, Tish?"

Tish agreed, but she couldn't have said what she was agreeing about.

"Unless there's something really weird," Megan said. "I'm not talking about Kipper, Tish, relax. Put your tray down. I'm thinking about Randy—I mean—if there was something — " her thoughts troubled her.

"Like what?" Jen wondered, and Angie, also, and Maria. "Like what?"

Tish didn't know how she felt about the turn the conversation was taking. She gripped both hands onto the bench, one on each side of her legs.

"If it was AIDS," Megan went on, "you know they probably wouldn't tell us. They'd say they were protecting us, because it would scare us or something."

"Well it would scare *me*," Judy said.

"Or if the baby's father was — like, a grown-up."

Tish couldn't believe she had said that.

"They wouldn't tell us about that, either. They, you know, stick up for one another, protect each other."

"What do you mean? Like, someone she baby-sat for? One of the fathers?"

"It's happened, baby-sitters and the fathers."

"But Randy didn't baby-sit, did she? She had to stay home and take care of her mother, remember? That was how she could miss so much school."

"Guess that leaves only *her* father," Tish joked. Ha, ha.

"Jesus, Tish."

"Even for you, that's sick."

"Too much Oprah Winfrey, Tish, it's gone to your brain."

"Besides, I heard it was stepfathers, mostly," Angie said.

"Just because people say things, that doesn't mean it's true," Maria said. "I mean, I don't know, don't most of us have stepfathers?"

Tish looked around.

Maria was saying something else, now, and Tish couldn't quite catch it, and everyone was nodding. Then Maria was asking something else, too, something sarcastic, and then Maria was sticking her elbow into Tish's side, to tell Tish to stop daydreaming.

Tish stopped daydreaming.

"The whole subject's gross," Angie said. "I wish you wouldn't even mention it."

Tish wasn't about to. She wouldn't, ever.

"Besides, isn't Randy's dad a social worker? He'd know better," Angie reminded them.

Chrissie stared at Angie. "You're kidding, aren't you? I hope you are. Do you think, doctors and teachers, therapists — you think only nonprofessionals commit crimes? Or incest?"

Tish admired Chrissie, who could say the word. Chrissie's smile commiserated with Tish. But, why?

"You're the ones who were calling things weird," Tish pointed out. "I was just giving the weirdest example I could think of."

"Don't do me any more favors," Danielle said.

Tish grinned and was pretty sure she looked real. There were still a few funny looks on some of the faces. "You don't know what you might be missing," she said, and when they stopped groaning she asked Chrissie, "What does your father say?"

Chrissie's father was always taking Issue Cases — affirmative action cases, child protection cases, equal housing and employment cases, what he called Marauding Caretaker cases against places like nursing homes or financial institutions. Chrissie's father often had an unusual slant on things and he apparently talked with Chrissie.

"He hasn't said anything about Randy, as a case," Chrissie said.

"Why don't we even give her her real name?" Tish demanded, and then clamped her teeth shut. If she was going to start yelling in the cafeteria, yelling at these people who thought they were her friends and thought they knew what she was like . . .

she thought, she was falling apart. She was going to fall apart, right here in the cafeteria.

"Miranda," Chrissie said nicely. "Tish is right, we can at least give her her real name. Dad, what Dad does is, he tries to sound me out, you know, being very subtle. It makes him nervous, a suicide makes everyone nervous. They don't know what to say or do."

"Isn't that the truth?"

Not the truth about all of them. Some of them knew just what they wanted to say, and do. And they said it. And they did it. Tish's jaw was tight.

"But there isn't even going to be a funeral." The words burst out of Danielle. "She's dead and she doesn't even get a funeral. And the school had that assembly, a day after, with the shrink — and that was it. It's as if she doesn't matter, and never did."

Tish wondered why it was that that made Danielle weep, and didn't ask. Some questions, when you asked them, people would wonder why those were the questions you asked.

"I'm just as glad," Angie said. "To be honest."

"Would you have gone to a funeral, Dani?" Tiffany asked. "I wouldn't have felt right, going. It's not as if I knew Randy, or was a friend of hers. It's not as if I liked her."

"But you used to, and so did I, and Tish, too, and you too, Judy," Megan said. "When we were in grade school, remember? I remember — she was someone whose tag team you wanted to be on, and jump rope, too. I remember sleepovers she came to."

"You may remember that kind of thing, but I don't. Don't get me wrong, I'm sorry she wanted to kill herself, but I can't believe I was ever friends with someone like Randy. I never would have."

"A lot of us were friends with her. There are lots of things children don't care about, and besides, I don't remember her being so creepy then. We were just children."

"You think we aren't still children?" Tish demanded. She didn't know what was making her so mad. "You're a fool, then, Megan, if you think that. It's pretty stupid not to know that."

She pushed herself up, and stood back, and walked away, her Docs clumping on the cement floor. *Dumb,* she thought, *dumb, dumb, dumb.* But she didn't know if she was talking about Megan, or about all of them, or about herself.

Anyway, she wasn't going to talk to anyone about Miranda any more. She didn't know what she might say next, if she started talking about Miranda. That was how to get nowhere. Fast. Talking about Miranda, talk and talk and it never made any difference.

Certainly not to Miranda.

Only *doing* something made any difference.

What, like putting a survival knife down on the table? Tish didn't want to think about the difference doing that might make.

Anyway, she wasn't just talking about Miranda anymore. She was doing something. Getting out of the cafeteria.

─Five─

Tish changed into shorts for gym but she kept the Docs on, with the survival knife hidden up against the outside of her right ankle.

She hadn't thought of that problem, or how to deal with it, the problem of gym and gym shoes. There were thirty-seven of them, thirty-seven girls filing into the gym and sitting down on bleachers, thirty-seven girls waiting to be sorted into drill teams, thirty-six of them in shorts and sneakers, one of them in shorts and Docs.

Coach Marchon saw it right away. Saw the Docs, or maybe she heard them. But she didn't say anything right away. Marchon didn't waste energy on words; she'd just say "Ten laps" and turn her back. Running laps was fine by Tish; she never minded laps. She wouldn't mind running ten laps, or even twenty, or even for the whole class. She waited to hear what she'd get.

The coach called out names, taking attendance. She explained the drill setup they'd be following. She sent people out to get started, counting off a line of seated girls with a pointing forefinger, then waving them onto the gym floor with a flick of her hand: off from the right, off from the left.

It didn't take Tish long to see how Marchon was going to handle this. She was going to get everyone else onto the floor doing something else, and isolate Tish, to keep it just between the two of them.

Tish figured, the fear she felt at her stomach had nothing to do with Marchon herself. Tish wasn't afraid of Marchon. It was something else she was afraid of, it was other things. Marchon couldn't know that, had no idea what was really going on — and that was just fine by Tish, even if it did get her into trouble.

"Those shoes, Tish," Coach Marchon said, at last.

Tish nodded, and stretched out her legs, bringing the Docs into prominence, crossing her legs at the ankles, which kept the outside of her right boot pretty much hidden.

"They're not allowed on this floor. You know that. They're *death* to gym floors, those soles."

Tish nodded up at the coach. Marchon looked down at her, then raised the whistle to her lips and blew it, to start things moving. The gym filled with the echoing sounds of bouncing balls and moving feet, and girls playing something: the quarrels and blamings, and laughter, and cries of dismay, and cries of exultation. Marchon had to raise her voice so Tish could hear her. "Where are your sneakers?"

Tish shrugged. "I took them with me yesterday. To wash them, because they stank, you know? I haven't washed them for, oh, weeks, since the end of the last marking period, I think. Which is a while back." She grinned like a fool.

Marchon waited.

Tish waited.

It was an old device — make *them* ask the questions.

Marchon was trying to see if she could get around the confrontation. She decided she couldn't — which just showed Tish which of the two of them was smarter, no matter who might have the college degree, and the teaching job, no matter who was the adult.

"You left your sneakers at home?" Marchon asked. "That's your excuse?"

"I never thought to check them in the dryer until just before I left," Tish said. "My mom's finishing them today. Sorry."

Sometimes she wondered why she lied so much at school, and to Kipper, too; but really she knew the answer. There was no other way she could think of. Sometimes she wondered why, in that case, she made such a thing about not-lying, to Tonnie or her mother, when it would make everything so much easier. "I didn't mean to," she said now, as loud as she could without yelling, to drive Tonnie out of her head.

Otherwise she might lose her grip on this present situation, and lose the knife, and lose her only hope of defending herself. She sat up, pulling her feet under the bench to hide them. "I'll have them tomorrow," she said, and didn't know if she would be able to keep her own word.

Marchon waited.

Tish waited.

She wasn't going to offer to borrow anyone's. She'd say she was worried about foot fungus. Marchon had no choice except to let Tish sit it out.

But the coach wanted to win this one. "I guess you'll have to play in your socks."

"I'm not wearing socks."

"Tish, I can *see* them. White cotton socks, I can *see* — "

Tish shook her head. "I can't."

"Can't what?" Marchon crossed the line over into being exasperated. "Well, *I* can't spend all period arguing with you. Take the boots off and I want you in" — she pointed — "Shantal's group, and I want you out there ASAP."

Tish shook her head.

"Why not?"

There wasn't anything Tish could say, it was too late to claim cramps or queasiness, what could she say? Because I've got a knife in my boot and if you know that, you'll confiscate it, and I won't have it when I need it, and I already told him I had it so if I don't have it . . .

Say that?

Tish couldn't say anything.

"I can't," she said again, in a voice that was so little, it surprised her. She swallowed back the words, *Please, please don't make me.*

Marchon stared at her. The noises of play and voices bounced around the gym. Marchon stared for a while, then said, "I wish you wouldn't do things like this, Tish. You've been working up to this for about a week, seeing how far you can push me. Yesterday was how far, Tish."

The coach crouched down and put both of her hands around Tish's left calf, to pull it out from under the bench, so she would be able to pull off the boot, to take it off Tish's foot no matter what Tish wanted. "I just wish you'd take a tenth of the energy you burn cooking up excuses and use it to pass gym. It would be easier on you. I wish you wouldn't force the issue until I have to — "

Tish couldn't breathe. The coach was a big woman, and strong, in good shape. She had no trouble getting the left leg out to where she wanted it.

Because the leg just gave up. The leg got strengthless, as soon as Marchon grabbed it, it never even tried, it was like some dead fish, flopping forward as soon as Marchon started pulling and she pulled it right out where she wanted it.

Tish was screaming.

She bent forward and grabbed on to her left leg to pull it back, out of Marchon's grasp. And screamed. Howled.

Her voice was the only sound in the gym. All other noises were shocked into silence.

Tish went on screaming, anyway. She couldn't have stopped even if she'd decided to. Any more than she had decided to start.

Marchon backed off, but Tish screamed. She wrapped her arms around her knees and pulled them in close to her chest — the right foot tucked away behind the left — and screamed.

She couldn't see anything, just the blinding red-and-yellow sound of her screaming.

Her eyes were closed.

She hadn't known that.

She opened them as wide as her mouth.

Faces all around, pale and worried, and now Coach Marchon was half-lifting Tish.

Tish felt her feet fall down and hit the ground. Her legs sort of straightened.

Her screaming by now had filled the whole huge gym with ricocheting sound, pitched high like missiles. Faces stared at

Tish, afraid, as if she was a nut case.

Tish tried to take a look at the nut case, which was her.

Laughter choked off screams.

Screams overrode laughter.

Tish was bent over a little.

They walked her right through the wide gym doors because some people were holding them apart. There was one person on each side of her, mumbling something. Tish choked and laughed, and every now and then a little bubble of a scream would come through.

They got her into the Health Room, which was just around the corner. The nurse was there, there was a kid lying asleep on one of the cots, and by then Tish had become alarmed and now she silenced herself.

Her ears rang with echoes — of her own screaming. Her throat felt raw. Her heart thudded in her chest.

In the silence, once she caught her breath, and tried to think about what had happened, and tried to think about how she could get out of it, she turned to Coach Marchon, and grinned, and took a bow. "Some show, dontcha think?" This would be *The Don't Mess With Me Show*, starring Tish.

Tish the performer, on stage, that's who

she was, Tish giving a show. Anything else was locked back up so deep inside her, nobody would ever find it out. Deep and safe and far from where anybody could get to her. Outside and onstage, Tish tossed her head and kept the grin on her face.

She couldn't have found the muscles to get rid of that grin, but there was no way for them to know that.

"I'm fine. Go on back," she told Angie. "It was a joke. Juh — juh — it was the J-word," she told Coach Marchon, grinning away like some skull. "I guess I went too far, hunh?"

"I'm going to have to talk to Mr. Sutterfield," Marchon said, stubborn, warning. "I don't know."

Right-on you don't, Tish thought, and grinned.

Inside she was bent over, sobbing, beaten for good. Lost.

"Is there anybody you'd like to stay here with you while you wait?" the nurse asked. Clearly, this wasn't a job the nurse wanted for herself. Tish's grin started to feel natural.

"I'm fine. I'm okay. There's nothing wrong, I'm just — if I could just stay here until the next period," she offered.

The nurse looked alarmed.

"I'm okay, honest," Tish said. And that *was* the exact momentary truth.

The truest thing she'd said in all of this, and it was a terrible lie.

"I could get Kipper. Or Chrissie, she always knows what to do. Or Mrs. Wyse? Mrs. Wyse might help," Angie said.

No surprise to find Angie horning right in on things.

"Would you? Have Mrs. Wyse paged for me?" Coach Marchon asked. "I've got a gym full of frightened girls. . . ."

Angie trotted off. Fetch, Angie, fetch. Angie was fetching. Tish giggled.

"She could wait in your office," Coach Marchon suggested to the nurse. "If you leave the door open. . . ."

They didn't think Tish could figure out what was worrying them. *What if she's out of control? What if she's having a psychotic episode? What if she kills herself? What if she starts smashing things, windows? What if she looks at the* records? *What if? What if?*

"Yes, all right," the nurse said. "If you insist. If you say it's all right. If you'll take responsibility."

"I won't be long," Coach Marchon said.

"I'm fine," Tish repeated, but she made

the mistake of yelling it, because they weren't even listening to what she was saying.

All this trouble, she thought, when all she was trying to do was be sure she didn't lose her survival knife.

And she hadn't, Tish thought, with an exultant smile that she was quick to hide.

—Six—

She was alone in the little office for maybe fifteen seconds, maybe as long as a whole minute. Not enough time to even begin to think of her next move. Barely enough time to say twice more to herself, "You still have the knife. You're okay. You'll be okay." Then somebody came to the door and needed dealing with. The feet just stood there in the doorway.

Tish didn't bother.

"Tish? What is this all about? Are you all right?"

It was Mrs. Wyse, and she asked the question as if it was her real question, not just the introduction to a Yes-answer from Tish.

Tish shrugged.

"Can I come in? I don't have to if you'd rather not."

"No, that's okay. I don't mind. I'm not — "

Mrs. Wyse smiled, sort of a little lifting up of one side of her mouth, ironic. "Oh, but you *are*," she said, and that almost made Tish laugh.

"I was watching you in class, smiling the way you smile, as if — It's so sad, Tish. When you smile."

Mrs. Wyse was nervous. She kept her face calm, but her hands were holding on to one another, clutching one another like little frightened children. Tish liked Mrs. Wyse fine and she didn't want her getting bent out of shape over Tish's problem. She tried a little joke. "Irony, right?"

"I think so." There was something Mrs. Wyse didn't want to say, but she was going to have to say it. "You'll be called to the office, Tish."

The ring of muscle at the top of Tish's throat tried to close up. She swallowed, to keep it open. "I figured."

She didn't dare ask Mrs. Wyse what she wanted to know about: What should I say? What can I do? Is there any way out, what's the way out?

"It's been a bad week for you, Tish. In behavior, at least, your grades seem to be fine."

"My grades are great. Honor roll, and sometimes high honors: okay, maybe not *great*, not like Alexander the Great, but pretty good."

"You've got some people pretty worried about you."

Tish wanted to ask, and didn't: What about you, are you that worried, worried enough to help?

"Probably," Mrs. Wyse said gently, "you'll see Mr. Sutterfield and Mr. Terry together. It was pretty scary just now — Coach Marchon said you were — out of control."

They didn't know the half of it, if they thought that was out of control.

Maybe Tish should just let go and really be out of control. Out of control. OOC. Ooc, oock. She could just let go of this body, and — like a balloon, when you filled it with air and then let go. Tish would go blatting backwards, around the room, and then either out the window and away or splat against a wall. And never mind anything else. It would all be decided for her, anyway.

"I guess, a little," Tish said. "I guess I overreacted."

"What are you up to, Tish?" Mrs. Wyse asked, her voice warm with patient good humor.

Tish looked up at Mrs. Wyse's face. Faded blue eyes, fading freckles, fading red hair — It was Mrs. Wyse's face, all right. Her throat spasmed again.

"Can I help?" Mrs. Wyse asked, and she sounded like she meant it.

Tish forced words out of her constricted throat. "Did you ever — I mean, before you grew up and got your own life, I mean, when you were a kid, little, did anything ever happen — anyone ever — and you couldn't do anything?"

Mrs. Wyse's worried eyes got more worried. The rest of her face, mouth and skin and all, got absolutely still. Her face turned into a mask, a face that was supposed to hide what she was thinking. To give herself time to think, behind the mask.

"Is this something about Randy?" Mrs. Wyse asked.

But she knew it wasn't.

Tish made herself try. "It's about — "

Mrs. Wyse looked at the open door, looking for help.

"You seem to understand," Tish pleaded, "so I thought, maybe something when you were little, before you were old enough, and you couldn't help yourself — "

"What are you saying?" Mrs. Wyse whispered.

Tish couldn't say it.

"How can you even suggest such a thing?" Mrs. Wyse whispered. "It's outrageous, Tish, you don't know anything about me, and you go saying — that isn't what people say about me, is it? You should be ashamed — "

"Sorry," Tish mumbled. "I'm sorry, I didn't mean — "

"Then maybe you'd better tell me what you did mean," Mrs. Wyse said, drawn up tall and away now.

"I'm sorry, I just — because my stepfather — "

Mrs. Wyse held up her hand. In stop position, to stop the words. "Wait."

Tish didn't want to be talking, anyway.

"Wait. Tish? Before you say any more."

No problem. Tish was at full stop.

Mrs. Wyse leaned back against the nurse's desk, beside Tish's chair, where Tish could see her profile. "Say anything to me, or to Mr. Sutterfield, or Mr. Terry, or to any of us, because I'm required by law— we all are — "

They weren't looking at each other, as if they were ashamed. They both whispered.

Mrs. Wyse said, "Listen."

There was danger all over the little room. The nurse's office was lit with long fluorescent bulbs, a sharp, bright light, but that couldn't even begin to drive the dark away, where danger hung invisible and horrible.

"Listen," Mrs. Wyse said again. "Wait."

Tish waited. Listening. She didn't know why she was listening when she already knew what was going to get said.

"Because sometimes — especially teenagers — we say things, when we're angry, or because we just — feel like we'll blow up if we don't. And usually it doesn't matter what we say, when we're angry. Because people know we're just angry. But some things — You can really do damage with some of the things you can say, Tish. You can really hurt people, and whole families, people you care for."

Tish felt her heart getting heavy —

Heavy, her heart sank, down onto her stomach, down into her belly, sinking, pulling her down behind it.

"You have to think about consequences, Tish."

What about my life? What about my consequences? a little voice inside Tish wanted to ask, but the voice was getting smaller and smaller, and if she opened her mouth to say something, she would weep, and cry. So all she could do was swallow down the tears and nod her head, just to stop Mrs. Wyse from talking anymore, and saying again what she had already said. Tish could barely stand to hear it once.

"I know what you're going to say, Tish, and I want to warn you, I'm not going to believe you," Mrs. Wyse said instead.

That sat Tish up. She looked at her teacher's profile. Mrs. Wyse was perfectly ordinary, and seemed pretty happy most days. She seemed to like kids, and she was fair, and she had two children of her own — both in grade school — and she had a husband who was the manager of one of the convenience stores. Sometimes you'd see them all shopping together. Or him taking her to the movies. Mrs. Wyse had a completely normal life.

So how could she know what Tish was going to say? There was only one way Tish could think of.

Tish wanted to ask, but didn't dare. Because Mrs. Wyse already denied even a hint. And because if Mrs. Wyse had gotten a normal happy life and was advising Tish not to say anything —

Tish didn't know if she had things wrong or right, she just didn't know.

"Once you start things happening," Mrs. Wyse explained, "you can't stop them. Whatever way they go, once they start, they keep going on, regardless of what you want. Because one of the people you are likely to hurt most is yourself, Tish."

Tish didn't need to ask how.

"When something like Randy happens in a school — Do you know what I'm trying to say? There's some funny kind of mass suggestibility that starts happening."

Tish nodded. Besides, she knew she wasn't thinking too clearly. Understatement of the day. She was afraid, in fact, that she was really getting crazy. Crazier by the minute, so she was pretty sure her guess about Mrs. Wyse was way off. If only because, if it ever happened to you, you couldn't tell someone else to keep her mouth shut. Could you? Because you'd know how bad it was.

And if anyone ever asked Tish, later, for

help, ever even just hinted, Tish would know exactly how that girl felt. And she'd *have* to help, if she knew.

" — warn you. No matter if it isn't her fault at all, when a girl gets a reputation, any kind of a reputation — you know? People accept only that reputation, once you've got one."

"Like Miranda?"

"Like Randy. Or Miranda, if that's what you think she'd like to be called. Because, randy Randy, isn't that what they called her? Once people found out — and even if what they found out had been false, it doesn't even matter if you're entirely innocent — "

Shame wrapped its red claws all around Tish, and squeezed. Choking her breath off. Cutting into her back and the back of her thighs. Red-clawed, red-hot shame wrapped itself around her, and every inch of her skin burned.

Tish tried to push shame away. With her hands. She wasn't innocent.

"Take a breath, deep," Mrs. Wyse spoke softly. "Out deeply. Again, Tish. Is that better?"

Tish nodded. She had the knife. She still had the knife. She was still okay.

"Are you ready to go to the office?"

Tish nodded. She barely heard the teacher's words.

"I'll walk you there," Mrs. Wyse said. "I can't stay, because I have a sixth-period class, and they'll rip the room up if I'm not there to leash them in."

Tish recognized the joke and pushed her mouth into a smile.

"But I'll go with you as far as I can."

Tish nodded. She guessed that was something.

"I hope everything works out, Tish," Mrs. Wyse said, and Tish knew then she had to be all wrong about Mrs. Wyse, because if she was right in her guesses, Mrs. Wyse could never say — and sound like she was sincere, sincerely hoping — that there was any hope that everything could work out. Tish didn't know *what* she could hope for. Just — maybe not to lose the knife.

Outside the office, Tish only got to wait about five minutes, sitting in a chair that curved around her back. The secretary typed away, long red nails clicking over the computer keys.

Tish used her five minutes for trying to figure things out.

Goals: Keeping the knife, that was the first.

That was the only one, too, because when she tried to figure out what else she wanted, there wasn't anything else. Just the knife, so she could protect herself.

She couldn't get her mind past the knife.

Okay, that was pretty clear and simple, and if that was all she wanted, then she was doing okay for now.

So, what could she say to Mr. Sutterfield, to explain the scene in gym? Maybe, if she said she'd tried a drug? Something — No, they'd do a urine test, so — maybe if she said PMS? Men were gullible about that; but all that screaming wasn't anything like normal, even for PMS, so that . . . maybe if she said that she'd tried LSD a while ago, last summer — off campus, out of the school season, nothing the school had to do anything about — and she'd had a couple of psychotic episodes since then?

Apologize, first, that was what she should do. That was what somebody normal would do. That was what somebody not in trouble would do. "I don't know what came over me. I'm so embarrassed," she silently rehearsed her lines. "Poor Coach Marchon, poor Mrs. Wyse, I don't know what they must think. They were so nice to me, and sympathetic," she said, in her head, and the imagined Mr. Sutterfield murmured in sympathy, wanting to be as well-liked as the teachers. .

Promise never to do it again, ever. And then make sure you were never caught out, caught up short, you never got yourself trapped again that way. So you never had to look around at whoever was screaming like a real crazy, and see it was you.

Find, for example, a place to hide the knife at school.

In a locker? But they did locker searches, but for drugs and guns and switchblades, she wondered if a survival kni —

"Tish?" The secretary held the phone to her ear. "Mr. Sutterfield can see you now. Yes, sir, she's right here waiting. She'll be right in, and I'll make that other call." Her fingers pressed down on the disconnect button, and Tish entered Mr. Sutterfield's office.

The principal wore a brown suit and a brown tie. He stood up behind his desk when Tish came in, as if she were a grownup; but he was proud of his old-fashioned manners, holding doors, shaking hands, saying Please and Thank You, calling the student body Ladies and Gentlemen, so there wasn't anything personal about him standing up, as if she were a grown-up. He barely dared to look at her, he was so afraid she'd start up at something again.

"Come in, please, Tish. Have a seat." Mr. Sutterfield came out from behind the desk to pull a chair forward for her. "Would you like to sit? Or would you rather stand, and perhaps look out the window?" His voice got loud then soft, loud again, then soft. He talked fast, and nervous. "I don't know, whatever, you can get in touch with nature, at the window."

"I'd like to sit, please," said Tish, the polite child. She sat, and folded her hands in her lap, and tucked her right Doc behind the left, just in case. She knew how to be a perfect polite child. "I'm awfully sor — "

But he was already seated and leaning forward across his desk toward her, and talking. "You caused quite a stir there in gym. Quite a stir, I must say. Coach Marchon is worried, and I've asked Mr. Terry to bring your file in, and join us. We're all worried about you, Tish."

That was all right, she could handle the counselor, she knew how to handle him, she could cope with both of those men. And what they were worrying about.

"If that doesn't strike you as too many of us?" Mr. Sutterfield asked. "And, would you like to have a woman present?"

"No, that's fine." It took more than those two to worry Tish, although she was trying to think of what might be in her record already, which they might think shouldn't be there. Like last year. Like her grades last year. Tish could explain last year's grades, she didn't know how, but she could explain, she was sure of it. She'd think of something.

"Good, good." Mr. Sutterfield was so relieved, he almost looked happy. "You do seem — calmer now. I must say. From what I was told. Are you feeling better? We really want to be able to understand what's going on, Tish."

"I am better," Tish said. "Really." Scared sober, that's what she was, only she was scared normal. To her own ears, trying to sound sincere and innocent made her sound false. She'd never believe herself if she heard herself talking in that sincere voice. Which made it lucky for her that she wasn't the person she was trying to convince.

His phone rang, and he said, "Do you mind?" to Tish, as if he'd only answer the phone if she said it was all right. But he gave her no time to respond. He had the receiver to his ear before she could have answered his question to say, "Yes, I do." If she'd cared.

"Yes," Mr. Sutterfield said. "Yes? Then call *him*," Mr. Sutterfield said. He replaced the receiver, and smiled across the desk at Tish.

She made herself sit still, still and calm.

Mr. Sutterfield studied her.

"We really do want to help you through this," Mr. Sutterfield said. "Whatever it is."

She thought that he meant what he was saying. She thought he was saying something he meant. "Yes, sir. I am sorry," she said.

"I know we make mistakes — we grown-ups — even with the best of intentions. I know that," and he smiled at her, like a kindergarten teacher smiling down on one of her five-year-olds. "The important thing for you to remember, Tish, is this. That we really do care about you. We care what happens to you. And we care how you feel."

He wanted her to believe him.

"Yes, sir," she said. "I'm sorry."

And within limits, she did believe him. And she did believe he meant what he was saying. That wasn't the problem, whether he meant what he was saying. The problem was Tonnie, and if she could keep herself safe from him. She wished school hadn't gotten into it — and she knew that was her own fault, but, still, she wished.

"I've put in a call to your mother," Mr. Sutterfield said.

Tish nodded. She was ready for that.

"Because I thought we should all talk together with Mr. Terry. Does that sound fair to you?"

"Yeah, sure."

He waited for more.

"That makes sense," Tish added.

"Good. I hoped you'd see it that way. The only question I have is whether you would like to be a part of the discussion. Do you think you would?"

Tish hesitated. How would somebody else answer? What would the normal response be, the one Angie or Chrissie would give, someone normal? She'd like to know what they were thinking about her, what she was up against, but she didn't want anyone thinking she wasn't exactly normal, unlike everybody else. She nodded her head slowly, ready to change her mind if he gave her clues that Yes was the wrong answer.

"We would certainly like to have your input in the discussion," Mr. Sutterfield said. "We believe students should take part in the important decisions about their lives. So as soon as Mr. Terry gets here — " he looked at his watch. He didn't know what to do with Tish until then. She could have laughed at how uncomfortable he was. He didn't know *what* she might do next, and that made him scared to be alone here with her.

" — and I've got a call in to your father, since your mother can't — "

Tish's whole body jerked to attention, and she needed all of her strength to hide the involuntary leap from Mr. Sutterfield. He was looking right at her, so she couldn't show a thing. She kept her eyes on his, and grabbed her left hand with her right hand, and bent her left little finger back, using her right-hand fingers to do it — it pulled a muscle on her arm, tight, and forced the joint back, sharply painful, and steadily, and every second a little more painful — she focused on the pain. "You mean my step-father," she said, her voice — even to her own critical ears — just slightly higher. But not shaking and howling, not giving away the way she felt.

"I thought he'd adopted you."

She nodded, agreeing.

"When you were very little, wasn't it?"

She agreed silently. She didn't dare open her mouth. She had to look calm, and stay still.

"So I always thought he was effectively your father. After all these years."

Tish tried to guess how long it would take Tonnie to get from work to school. And kept bending her finger back.

"Especially since you haven't seen your birth father since you were one — except" — he looked down at an open file on his desk — "once, for one week, when you were five." Mr. Sutterfield smiled at her, pleased with himself. At that moment, his phone buzzed and he picked it up. "Sutterfield here," he said, and he listened. "Yes, well, I'm sorry to disturb you, but it's Tish — she's right here in the office with me. There was — an episode, in gym class."

Mr. Sutterfield listened. Tish guessed she knew who he was talking to, and when Mr. Sutterfield sort of chuckled at something the phone said, she thought she could guess what he was being told.

"Yes, well, you could say that about her, and I'd have to agree," Mr. Sutterfield said. "Of course you can take her home with you, that would be best all around. I'm grateful that you're being so understanding. You'll be right over, then?"

Mr. Sutterfield was smiling to himself as he hung up the phone. "You kids don't know," he said to Tish, the smile leaving his face.

"No, sir," Tish said.

"How lucky you are."

"Yes, sir."

"To have people willing to drop everything. And be responsible for you. He said to tell you not to worry, he'll be right down to straighten things out."

Tish nodded. She tried to guess how much longer she had before Tonnie walked in through the door.

"And take you home with him. He said if he were a lawyer, he'd advise you not to say a word until he got there. To let you know what it was all right for you to say."

Tish wished he were a lawyer, she could probably use a lawyer in her life, ha, ha. She didn't need to guess about what was all right to say. And what wasn't. Nor about how Tonnie'd act while they were in the principal's office. Or later. The only question was, how long it would take for later to arrive, and Tonnie started getting even. Once he had her inside his house.

Tish didn't think she could sit in that chair and watch Tonnie walk through the door.

She thought she would faint. She thought she might faint just *thinking* about it, and waiting for it to start happening. She had really done it to herself this time, hadn't she?

"Do you call him Dad?" Mr. Sutterfield asked.

She nodded. Fear vibrated around inside her head. It didn't matter what she said.

Then — like a gun going off, hope.

"So you must have warm feelings about him, maybe even better than kids have about their real fathers," Mr. Sutterfield said.

"May — " Tish took a breath, licked her dry lips. "Sir? I have to go to the bathroom."

He looked at his watch.

"I won't be long," she offered.

"I'm not sure," he said, doubting.

"Sir — I *have* to," she urged.

Time, that was all she needed. And not much of it, either. All she needed was enough time to get out of the building. But she didn't want to alarm Mr. Sutterfield. If she alarmed him, he wouldn't let her leave the office, or he'd insist someone go with her, and they were on the ground floor but the bathroom windows were set high in the cement block walls, and only about six inches wide.

"Well, in that case," Mr. Sutterfield said.

"But you won't be long, will you?" He stood up, good-mannered.

"Oh, no, I won't," she promised. Then she was out of his office, and out of the anteroom, and out in the hall, where nobody could see which way she went or how fast.

—Seven—

They were chasing her, and she couldn't run any faster. Tish crashed on down the walk that went to the street. If she could just make it to the street, she'd be safe. They couldn't drag her back into the building, could they? If she could just get off school property, she'd be out of their jurisdiction.

Wouldn't she?

It was like running in a dream. Her feet felt slow and heavy. Her heart thudded and her chest ached, as if she had been running for a mile, or two, or five.

Was this some dream? And she hadn't even woken up?

And she was going to have to do it all again? Face Tonnie at breakfast —

Tish didn't know if she could come up with the strength to do that again. She couldn't do that again.

And what was wrong with her that a one hundred-yard sprint — it wasn't any more than that, at all, if barely — had her breathing so hard? Heart pounding against her chest and in her ears. Heart pounding.

Footsteps, running, behind her — two pairs, four feet, both hitting the ground lightly. Should she turn to face her pursuers? To fight them? With the survival knife?

Because when she lost, they'd take the knife away, and that would be that. Sooner or later, that would be that for her.

Her Docs felt heavy. To lift. It seemed as if her feet stuck. To the cement walk like fly feet sticking to flypaper.

It seemed like a dream.

But she knew it wasn't.

And she wondered if she was crazy now. If she had stumbled over some edge — when she watched Mr. Sutterfield talk to Tonnie on the phone? — or if she had disconnected from herself in some unfixable way, last night? — If screaming like that in gym meant that from now on she was a nutcase, a loony tunes? She could still hear those screams, inside of her head, and they sounded pretty loony tunes to her.

How bad would that be, anyway? Being crazy. Never having to be sane again, never having to know what was happening to you. That didn't sound too bad.

What sounded bad was the footsteps. And the hand wrapped around her arm, jerking her back, around, pulling.

But she'd made it to the street. They couldn't —

Tish turned, in a fury. Teeth bared.

It was Chrissie, Chrissie was saying something. " — matter? Why are you — "

Tish bent over, trying to breathe. She braced her arms stiff against the hands she braced just above her knees. Gasping for breath. Chrissie talked on and on. Tish couldn't hear all of the words. " — heard and I — help — " Tish labored at breathing. " — look terrible."

Tish straightened up and looked terrible. It didn't work.

Then Kipper put his arm around her shoulder. "Tish? What's going — ?"

She shoved his hand away, and stood back from them both.

" — sorry — " Kipper said and she stopped hearing him. " — sorry — sorry — "

"She can't — " Chrissie said.

Tish was alarmed now. She couldn't speak.

" — help — " Chrissie said. "Come back — Dad — "

She might not be able to speak, but she could still say no. Tish shook her head, so hard her ears rang with it.

" — alone — " Kipper's mouth said.

That was for sure, Tish thought, as her head swung back and forth — No, No, No, No, No, No, No. No. It felt so good to be saying No, she didn't want to stop, even if she could have. No. No. No.

Chrissie punched her in the stomach.

Tish froze in place, instant statue, hands at her side. Waiting. For Chrissie's next move.

" — sorry — " Chrissie said. And looked to Kipper for help.

" — leaving — " Kipper said.

"Come — help you — " Chrissie said, and pulled on Tish's arm.

Something about that, something about being pulled at, and back toward school — Tish didn't know what she was doing, only her hands were tearing Chrissie's hands off her, and pushing Chrissie away, and knocking her down onto the sidewalk. Flat down hard on her pretty face, with a muffled thunk when her forehead hit the cement.

Tish took off, without another thought.

Let Chrissie get herself up and out of there by herself. Thinking she'd be able to catch Tish, and make her go back to Mr. Sutterfield's office, and wait for Tonnie to show up and take her away with him at the end. Let Chrissie have Kipper, too; he'd already joined up with her to catch Tish. They could have each other, and welcome to them.

She didn't care. She didn't care about either of them. Or anything else, either. Just getting out of there before Tonnie got there.

Tish ran. She ran along sidewalks and around anybody who happened to be walking on the sidewalks. She ran around corners and past houses, past stores. Running away. She ran until she couldn't run anymore, and then she sat down by the side of the road and put her head down against her knees. Her feet hurt. Running in Docs was no fun.

Now what? her brain asked.

But she had the knife. Right there in her right boot, right where she could get at it in a flash. So everything was fine.

Now what?

Her breath still hurt a little, though, and

her ears still rang. She'd better sit a little
longer before —
    Before what?
    Now what?

    There were tears in her mouth. She didn't
know. What else she could do. She was
going to have to go back to Tonnie's house.
She was going to have to go back because
there wasn't anything else she could do.
Even though she knew what was going to
happen when she got there.
    Or happen later.
    Sooner or later.
    Sooner and later.
    What had made her think she could get
away with getting away?
    She shouldn't have tried with Kipper,
either — even though he was sweet and
pretty funny, too, and cute, and said he liked
her. She believed him, but she should have
known she couldn't have a boyfriend. That
if she did, he'd get tired of her and change
to someone more normal, easier, someone
nicer, like Chrissie. Or if she did, she'd have
to get rid of him before he started to matter
too much to get rid of. Or if she did, sooner
or later he'd look at her just the way Kipper
just had.

Like someone who has had all he can take.

And say what Kipper just said.

She wiped at her face with her hand, and the palm came away wet, so she dried it on her arm. But she didn't have the strength to stand up.

Which didn't matter much, anyway.

What was it Kipper had just said, looking sad as some spaniel? Then turned away? She couldn't remember, just that it had to be the end of him, now that he knew she wasn't the person he thought she was.

And even *that* — what he saw and walked away from, the loony tunes, the shrieking crazy — wasn't as bad as she really was, wasn't even the bottom truth. If Kipper saw the bottom truth, she couldn't even imagine what she'd do.

She couldn't imagine what she could do even now. There didn't seem to be anything to do except go back. Or she could get herself sent to jail — maybe she could break into someone's house or a store and get herself sent to jail? — but not without her parents' consent, pretty much, not without them being involved, and that meant time at the house — waiting for the trial — and lawyers.

Chrissie had said something about lawyers, but Tish couldn't remember what.

So she was left with maybe turning tricks, except the difference between that and Tonnie wasn't something she could tell.

Which left her with only the obvious choice.

Which right that minute didn't look too bad.

Not nearly, for example, as bad as going back.

Chrissie had said something about Battle Link, whatever that was.

Miranda's choice: That was the only choice Tish had. She thought she knew how bad Miranda felt — and she could imagine how Miranda felt about that baby.

Tish believed in that baby. It was growing in Miranda, feeding on her body, getting bigger every day. It would be like having cancer, only worse. Cancer killed you off in pain, but this baby — this baby of Miranda's — would be hers to take care of for years and years. Miranda wouldn't even get to die, once the baby was born; once the baby was born, she would have to take care of it, and not know what might happen to it — what if the baby had it as bad as Miranda did? If Tish had a baby, she could imagine the things Tonnie might say; and do; and she knew she'd be trapped for her life then, with him, and it would be her own child that trapped her, and what if she loved it?

Because Tish knew Tonnie loved her.

Not love, her brain told her. Unless love is — everything that makes things worse, that breaks them down, and hurts.

Yeah, well, maybe that was a point.

And he said it was Tish's fault, anyway, making him love her.

And maybe it was. How did she know? Maybe there was something she did, without knowing, without wanting to. Maybe Tonnie was exactly what love was.

So, she needed to find something quick, something that would off her. Quickly.

Or go back and try to make it to eighteen. Just eighteen, and then she would be legally on her own. But she knew Tonnie, and she knew she'd gone too far that morning.

He liked being fought against when he knew he could win.

He liked being fought against because it meant he could do even more of what he wanted.

Tish's ears roared, as if wind blew around her, and her skin shrank up tight. She wished war would break out, right then, so she'd be safe. If war broke out and the whole world blew up, she'd be dead and safe from Tonnie.

The backs of her thighs shrank up, and the muscles under the skin tingled, all the way down to her knees.

Little moans crept out of her mouth.

She hated those noises, hated herself for whining, hated it.

Something about trouble, and the law, trouble and a lawyer, that was what Chrissie was talking about.

And where Chrissie got off threatening Tish . . .

Tish didn't need Chrissie to tell her she was in trouble. To remind her of the law.

It was like trespassing. The law about no trespassing. Like families had No Trespassing signs posted all around them.

At least she still had the survival knife.

That was the only thing she had. And she didn't know how much help she could hope for from it.

It had seemed like such a good idea, at the time.

It had seemed, when she was buying it and thinking about his face when she pulled it out under his nose and jammed it up against his throat — except she'd hidden it at the back of a drawer — which was so stupid, almost as if she didn't *want* to be able to defend herself, almost as if she wanted Tonnie. . . . Which was what Tonnie said, anyway, wasn't it, she was getting what she wanted, she was getting what she deserved: Tish's mind tumbled spiraled down and dark and she grabbed it where it careered off, and held it steady, pointing like a flashlight at the knife.

So the knife wasn't there when she needed — it had seemed to be all she needed, to take care of herself. That, and the truth — to get out from under all the lies. Get out from under Tonnie. Now it seemed she'd only made everything worse, using those two weapons.

She hadn't thought things could get worse.

Yeah, well, now she knew better, didn't she.

Served her right, anyway, didn't it. Tonnie would say that. And it began to seem to Tish that Tonnie was right. About her. About everything.

If Tonnie was right —

Tish was imploding, into a darkness so small and far away, and Tonnie could be right until all the seas ran dry, for all it made any difference to her.

Just a snot-faced girl sitting beside the road.

One of those cars, going by at forty-five or fifty, that would be quick.

If Tonnie was right, then all Tish wanted
was to die quickly, before he could ever get
his hands on her again.

As if she wanted to be obliterated.

To throw everything away, get rid of it
all, her hands and her legs, and the taste of
an orange. And all the days other people got
to live in without being — ashamed. Afraid.

Tish could almost see herself hanging on
Miranda's tree. Hanging naked there, because naked was the way to do it, the only
clean way to be sure. Only Tish wouldn't
pack any suitcase. She'd know dead was
gone for good, your one chance finished.
Flushed down the toilet. Your one and only
chance at life up in flames forever.

How could something as terrible as
Miranda's tree be so tempting?

If there was something worse than terrible, it could be.

Staying alive — hurt so bad — dying
looked — comfortable — Tish watched a
car go by, east, blocking her vision of the
van traveling west, and she could imagine
herself standing up, to dive onto the road,
and be a roadkill.

It was either that, or go back to Tonnie's
house, and let him be right.

Tish was afraid for herself.

When she was so much more afraid of

what the survival knife would let Tonnie do — to her — than of what Tonnie did — to her —

— that she'd rather be a dead person —

Battle, Inc. Inc for incorporated. That's what it was. Chrissie's father's law office, sort of a funny name for a lawyer, although not a bad one for a soldier — but what was Chrissie doing telling Tish that? They weren't friends, Tish barely knew Chrissie at all — although they'd been in school together from second grade, with Miss Hancock, and her pearl brooches, so Tish had known Chrissie a long time, even if they weren't friends — which wasn't Chrissie's fault, Chrissie was pretty friendly, it was just that Tish didn't have any friends. Not who might offer what Chrissie had offered, "Go talk to my dad." She'd said something more, too, something like, "My dad might be able to help." Something like that.

But how could Chrissie know Tish needed help?

Kipper, did Kipper tell her? But what did Kipper know about Tish? Nothing. Nobody knew anything about her.

Tish didn't even know where this Battle, Inc., was. She didn't even know Chrissie's father.

She could find a phone, and a phone book, and the number, and call him up. But she wouldn't know what to say. She wouldn't know how to tell, over the phone, if he was someone she could say anything to.

Just thinking about saying the words — her throat closed up.

And he had secretaries, too, she bet, she was willing to bet on that. A lawyer would, and she'd have to convince the secretary to let her talk to Chrissie's dad —

She didn't want to make any phone call. There was no point in even bothering with a phone call. She was kidding herself, trying to kid herself into thinking she wouldn't have to —

She could find a phone, and a phone book, and look up the address. Then she could put off even thinking about going back to Tonnie's house; or what she was going to do about her life if she didn't.

Putting off deciding about having to go back was reason enough to get her up onto her feet, and set her on her way to see if she could find where Chrissie's Dad worked. At Battle Link.

Finding wasn't the same thing as having to actually go in, or talk to anyone. Besides, Tish thought, if she did find the office and they were lawyers, maybe they could settle one question for her: maybe someone there could tell her what happened to a girl who attacked her adopted stepfather with a knife.

—Eight—

Tish found the address without any trouble — it was listed on one of the pages that hadn't been ripped out of the phone book in the first pay phone she came to. She found the office easily — up a set of outside stairs, over a fabric store. She watched her hand reach out for the brass doorknob, and turn it. Inside, a secretary worked at a desk, in a square room with the windows open. He finished up whatever he was doing on the computer before he turned to her.

He seemed surprised to see her.

Well, Tish figured, she sure didn't look like she belonged here at Battle Link, with its thick carpet and flowered curtains, with the pictures of streams running through hills at different seasons of the year. In her gym shorts and her Docs — and she didn't even want to think of what her face probably looked like, so she didn't — Tish couldn't blame the secretary for the expression on his face.

"Yes?" he asked.

"I'd like to see Mr. Battle," she said, standing in front of the desk as if she were in second grade or something. "If I can, please."

His face understood something, and he got ready to speak. She figured, he was going to find an excuse to get her out of the office.

"I don't have an appointment, but it's sort of an emergency, and Chrissie told me he might — that's his daughter, I mean, and it's not exactly an emergency, not life and death — " But all at once it didn't seem worth it. Just. Not. Worth. The effort. None of it was any use, anyway, and she didn't think she could face hearing from somebody else that there wasn't anything she could do. She already knew that. She knew it already. Knew it all over her body. It was only her heart that wouldn't lie down and give up.

What heart? Tish hadn't thought she had any heart left. But she knew, somehow, it was her stupid heart, saying *No,* saying, *Liar,* saying, *I can too.*

That heart was so stupid and stubborn, Tish practically fell in love with it, if that was possible, to fall in love with your own heart. Because it was on her side.

She didn't know whether to be angry at or grateful to her heart — she was so glad to know it wasn't dead.

Yet.

Just dying.

"Never mind, I'm sorry to bother you, I don't — " she was saying to the secretary, as she turned away from the expression on his face; because her heart was weak and she needed to protect it, because it was all there was good left of her, and anything she did to keep it safe was permitted. Anything at all.

"Wait," he was saying.

Tish set her feet down square on the thick rug. She was concentrating on keeping her fingers resting on her heart, holding on to her heart. She didn't know what had made her come to Battle Link anyway.

Because Chrissie told her to. Chrissie had to have some real leadership qualities if she could get Tish to do what she said. That thought almost made Tish smile.

The secretary spoke into the phone. "The

young lady to see you, sir." He nodded encouragingly at Tish, and rose out of his chair as he set the phone back on its cradle. "Can I get you a cup of tea? Or a soda?"

Tish was too tired even to try to smile back at him. She was so tired. . . .

"I'm not thirsty," Tish said. She didn't know whether she should leave or not. She didn't know where the worse danger lay, here or away from here. She'd made so many choices and decisions in the day, she couldn't even keep track of them, or keep them straight enough to know which ones worked, and which just made things worse.

Tish remembered something. "Thanks, anyway." She wasn't sure yet what she remembered, but she thought she probably would. And it would be important, and make everything clear. At the moment she was about to fly apart. There was some heavy, slow, slowly rising-up feeling in her, as deep and dark — like a picture of a tidal wave, so it wasn't flying apart she had to worry about, it was getting dragged up, drowned off. She headed for the door.

Next thing she knew, the door at the other end of the room opened, and a man hurried out. He looked calm and in control, sort of plump and successful, just the way

Chrissie's father should look, in a dark gray lawyer suit.

Chrissie's father stared back at Tish.

He looked like the kind of man things wouldn't go wrong on. Things wouldn't even want to go wrong on him, but if they happened to, he'd just get them back in order, without even taking his jacket off.

If this man was your father, then you'd have plenty of time to spend on studying, and sports, and dances, and having sleepovers. Tish was jealous of Chrissie, so jealous she could have howled.

But Chrissie said her father didn't know when she was lying.

And Chrissie's mother had gone off with some boyfriend. So he wasn't perfect, he couldn't be, or she wouldn't have run off.

Tish looked at him again, trying not to kid herself. You couldn't ever tell what was really there, behind the surface of people. His eyes were dark, and there seemed to be somebody smart and alive behind those eyes — and curious, too, and unsure of what to say. She could see Mr. Battle hesitate, wondering.

"Will you come into my office?" he asked her then. "Did Ian offer you something to drink?"

"She said she wasn't thirsty," the secretary said.

"I bet we could persuade her to have some lemonade," Mr. Battle said, smiling, warm but not crowding. Just as if he expected to enjoy the time he spent with her.

Tish was sorry. She shouldn't have come here. It wasn't anything to do with him. It wasn't the kind of thing he'd want anything to do with. "I'm sorry," she said.

"Already? Just a minute ago you looked like you wanted to punch my teeth in."

"I was thinking about something else," Tish said, and found that she had followed him into an office. There was a desk with two chairs facing it. There was a sofa with a chair beside it. Mr. Battle sat on the sofa.

Tish took the chair. She rested her hands on its thick arms. It was the same brick-red fabric as covered the sofa, rough against her palms.

To start with, they sat without saying anything. He was busy. He put a long yellow legal pad on the low table in front of him, and wrote something on the top of the paper with a pen. He shook the pen, and wrote again. He dropped that pen onto the table and took out another. That one pleased him. He looked at his watch and wrote another line.

Tish lined her feet up side by side. She folded her hands in her lap.

Mr. Battle straightened up and sat back, with the pad and pencil waiting on the table.

The secretary put a tall glass with ice and pale yellow liquid in it down on the table beside Tish. He put a mug down in front of Mr. Battle. He left the room, pulling the door closed behind him.

Mr. Battle smiled again. Tish looked away from his smiling, smooth-shaven face, looked out a window. He said, "I'm Ted Battle, Chrissie's father." He reached out to shake her hand.

She thought her palms were wet, and awful, but she had to shake because otherwise — why otherwise? she thought, what otherwise? So she dried her palms on her shorts and reached out her right hand.

"Tish," she introduced herself. She wasn't sure what she wanted to tell him.

"Chrissie said you might come by. She called me. What can I do for you, Tish? Chrissie didn't say."

"She called you up?"

He nodded, then picked up his coffee while Tish stared at him.

"From school?"

"She wanted to be sure, if you showed up, I'd know you were coming."

"Oh," Tish said.

She picked up her glass and drank some lemonade.

"That was nice of her," Tish said.

"Nice is Chrissie's middle name," he answered, so smoothly she knew it had to be a family joke about Chrissie.

"What do you think her middle name *should* be, then?" Tish asked, curious.

Now he looked surprised.

She wished she hadn't spoken. She didn't know it was something she shouldn't say. But before she could apologize, he was answering.

"Nobody has ever called me on that. Not even Chrissie," he said, and smiled again. "Now that you mention it, *Nice* might be just what it should be."

"It should," Tish agreed.

"Your disapproval is noted," he said.

"That was hope," Tish quarreled. And shut herself up.

Something about this office, and the cool drink, and the man himself — sort of unexcitable — got through to Tish, and made her relax. It made her nervous to feel so relaxed. She didn't know what she might say, or do, feeling relaxed. She sat up straight again, lined her feet up again.

He was watching her face. "What's the

trouble, then?" he asked. "Can you tell me?"

Words logjammed her throat. She shook her head, she couldn't speak.

"Chrissie didn't know, she just thought — she thought you might be in some kind of trouble."

Tish stopped her head from shaking back and forth, denying it, but she couldn't get a Yes out of her mouth. She couldn't get a Yes up through the cramped ring at the top of her throat.

He waited for a while, to give her a chance to answer him, then he changed the subject. "What do you know about me? I mean, the kind of work I do. You know I'm a lawyer, but what else do you know?"

"Not" — Tish cleared her throat. "Not much. Just" — she cleared her throat again — "just some of your cases — Chrissie says, and — I don't know what she told you, but it's not as if I'm a close friend of Chrissie's."

"I figured that. Although I've heard your name. Who *are* your close friends?"

Tish shook her head, shrugged.

He waited.

"Nobody," she said. "Not — nobody."

"Not even a boyfriend? Kipper, isn't it?"

Why would he know about Kipper? "Yes, but he's not — "

Mr. Battle thought about it. "So you're pretty much a loner?"

That was it, exactly. "Yes."

He looked up, then, as if she'd said something alarming. But she hadn't. So maybe she'd said it in a funny voice? She tried to hear in memory what her voice had sounded like, but she couldn't. Its echoes had already left the room. She couldn't tell what he might be thinking now, so she added to the Yes, "Pretty much. But I don't get lonely."

"No, of course not."

It was her turn to look carefully at him. She didn't think he was being sarcastic, but she wanted to be sure, because if he *was* being sarcastic, she was out of there. There was some tone in his voice, some carefulness in the way he agreed with her, that she wasn't sure about.

"I *don't,*" she insisted.

"Because you always *are,*" he said. "That's just a guess, but — I'd be surprised to hear that you have close friends," he said. "Or anyone close. I hope you don't think I'm being intrusive, or unkind? Nosy, judgmental, any of those things. I'm just trying to give you my first impressions. I'm trying to be open with you. Because I'm beginning to think Chrissie's got it right. Doesn't she? Aren't you in trouble?"

Tish was shaking her head No, not unkind, and nodding it Yes, she understood about first impressions, so she just went ahead nodding.

"I'm sorry," he said.

Tish believed him. She believed his voice and his words. There was no *but* attached to his sorry, like a dog jerked along at the end of a leash. He really was sorry things weren't going right for her. Tears filled her eyes. Tears filled her eyes up to the brim. Tears filled her eyes up to the brim and spilled over down her cheeks.

She shook her head, to clear her eyes, to get herself angry so the tears would stop.

They wouldn't stop.

So she got up out of the chair and put her back to him, moved over to a window and looked out. A parking lot, black asphalt, nine parking places, four of them — she held her shoulders stiff, so stiff they hurt. She just wanted to get in control, and then get out of there.

She heard Mr. Battle moving around, and then a box of tissues came over her shoulder. She took it.

"That wasn't nice of me," he said. "It

was thoughtless. I'm sorry, Tish. I should have said *I'm not a bit sorry, I expect whatever trouble you're in, it's your own fault.* That would've been easier on you, wouldn't it?''

Tish smiled to herself. Yeah, it would have been.

He was keeping back, away from her. She wondered if he knew how high she'd jump if he came any closer. ''How do you know — ?'' were all the words she could get out between tears.

''You know that Chrissie's mother left us?''

Tish nodded, mopping at her eyes and face, glad he hadn't understood what she meant to ask. Or maybe she wasn't glad. She didn't know. She couldn't stop the tears, but she stopped the heaving and gulping.

''Well, that was all years ago,'' he said. ''I was younger then,'' he said. ''With less experience.''

She wondered why he was delaying saying whatever he was going to say, why he'd do that.

''I thought, then, that some things mattered a lot that now I don't think matter very much at all,'' he said. ''And I had less experience of myself, too, of who I am, and what I can trust myself to take care of," he said. "I just didn't know as much as I do now."

He was looking out the window while he was speaking, now, and out of the watery corner of her eye she could see him decide to go on with saying it, whatever it was.

"When she left me, I remember feeling — it was easier not to break down — or crack up — to keep control, anyway, if nobody gave me sympathy. Feeling how hurt I was was the worst thing I could do to myself, letting myself feel abandoned and betrayed. Even though she had done just that, betrayed me, abandoned us. But, see, if it was *me*, if it was my fault, if I was a bad husband, boring, disappointing, unlovable, unloving, whatever flaw — if it was me that was wrong, I could *do* something about it. So I always preferred blaming myself. It took me a long time to be able even to say it: She did this to the children, and to me. If I hadn't had the children, I might have been stuck there. Unable to change and get free. But I was lucky, I had children, and I couldn't leave them there. In the victim place."

She was pretty much following him. He finished, and she looked over at him, trying to think if she should say she was sorry. She was, but she didn't know if she was supposed to be feeling that.

Then he looked at her, "You don't have children," he told her.

She shook her head, agreeing. And she thought: She might just tell Mr. Battle. She might be able to tell him. She waited for him to start guessing, so all she would have to do was nod Yes when he named it.

Wasn't there a fairy tale where the queen had to get the right name for the monster, or he would take her baby away?

If she just didn't have to say it, she'd be grateful for that.

Rumpelstiltskin, that was it.

As long as nobody named it, it might not be true.

Who would believe her, anyway?

Mr. Battle wasn't saying anything. She wished he would say something.

Like who would have believed the girl when she told them that it was a funny little monster man who spun straw into gold — because her father had lied to the king about her. Tish started to remember the story. The girl's father had lied about her, and the king said he'd cut off her head if she couldn't spin straw into gold. Which of course she couldn't do.

Mr. Battle had sat down again. He wasn't going to guess, he wasn't going to say anything, he was going to make her choose.

As if, Tish thought — from behind a curtain of tears — it was easy to believe a girl could spin straw into gold, but unbelievable that a funny-looking little monster man would come along to do it for her and then blackmail her.

She walked back toward Mr. Battle. He was going to *let* her choose.

That was a terrible story. The girl-queen couldn't do *anything*, between her father and the king and Rumpelstiltskin. Between them, they had her whole life to chew on, and her baby's life, too.

Tish thought, if she had to go on feeling helpless and hopeless, she'd rather be dead. She thought, in the story, it was a hunter who followed the little man and discovered his name, so the queen could save her child. The queen couldn't even save her own child, there had to be a hunter who felt sorry for her because she was sad and beautiful.

She thought, all those men, and the queen could only sit there among them, keeping her secrets from everyone; she couldn't *do* anything, just what they made her, or let her.

Tish thought, being alive and *doing* things,

they were about the same thing, and she reached down into her boot and pulled out the knife and set it on the table. Because she wanted a chance to have her life.

Mr. Battle looked at the knife. Uneasy.

She'd see what he said. She'd wait and see.

Tish stared down at the survival knife, where it lay on the table.

"That's a serious knife," Mr. Battle said.

Tish nodded, mopped at her face. She spoke from behind tears, still, but that didn't seem to bother her. "It's for Tonnie."

"Tonnie?" he asked.

"My father. Actually, my stepfather. Actually, he adopted me, when I was two, so he's my real father, I guess."

Mr. Battle didn't say anything, but all the things he was thinking and wondering filled the air of the room. He didn't even know if he could believe Tish, either — she knew that, and she knew it made sense, but she hated it, too.

She hated the way if she looked at his face, she'd see how it had turned into a mask, to hide what his thoughts were. She could just imagine what he might be thinking.

So maybe she was glad his face turned into a mask.

"I take it that the knife isn't a present," Mr. Battle said.

If she hadn't been weeping — standing there with her feet planted stiff against the floor to keep her legs from shaking — Tish would have laughed. You could look on the knife as a present, special for Tonnie. You might say it was a special kind of present, from Tish to Tonnie.

"If I — hurt him. If — if I kill him, even? What would happen to me?"

"That depends," Mr. Battle said slowly, and carefully, "on why you might have done it."

"Oh." Tish had said about all the words she could get out. Any more and she would be in serious trouble. Any more, and things that might not be believed — things that she might be saying not because they were true, but because her family might be right and she might be nothing but a crazy person who thought things that didn't ever happen had happened, and a liar, too, because she hated Tonnie enough to tell any lie that would get rid of him —

She knew that about herself, how much she hated him, so she couldn't deny that.

Then why should anyone believe her?

And, besides, if she said anything, things

would start happening about it. Until she spoke, they wouldn't.

And besides, until she spoke its name, it didn't have to be true. It could all be false and it wouldn't have to be true.

And, besides, this wasn't any fairy tale, because if she named it, it wasn't going to stamp its foot on the floor and disappear forever. Its name wasn't Rumpelstiltskin.

"If there *is* a reason," she said.

"If there is one, then what would happen to me?"

He didn't know the answer. She could see that in his face. Because his face wasn't a mask, if she dared to look at it, to see what he might be thinking. She wondered what he would say, when he didn't know an answer. It was important, what he chose to say.

"I don't know, Tish," he said.

She had to lock her knees to keep from collapsing onto the floor in relief.

"Juvenile center, foster home, psychiatric ward — that's what the institutions of society offer you. I'd do my best for you."

She didn't understand.

"As your lawyer," he said. "Do you have any money?"

She didn't understand, why should he need money? But she thought he was telling the truth and so she ought to answer him.

"A couple of dollars, probably."

"Give me a dollar, okay?"

Baffled, she reached into her pocket and pulled out the change, counting out a dollar in quarters and dimes and nickels. He stood up, shook her hand, took the money. "That makes you a client. Officially. Now anything you tell me is privileged information, confidential."

Tish understood. But she didn't think she could tell him any more than she had. She wasn't even sure she wanted to. She reached down to pick up her knife. "Thank you," she said.

At least she'd stopped the crying. Her voice was still thick, but she wasn't crying tears anymore, and the thick voice would fade pretty quickly.

"Wait. Tish? Was that all you needed from me?"

Needed, if he wanted to talk about need.

But he didn't, he had his own life, his own problems, and who wanted hers, anyway?

Nobody, that's who.

And Tish didn't blame anybody about that. Even she didn't want her own troubles. She wouldn't even wish them on her worst enemy.

Except Tonnie. She'd wish them on Tonnie.

"Thank you for talking to me, and answering my question," she said to Chrissie's father, and put the knife back in her boot. "Thank you for saying you'll be my lawyer."

"If you need one. I have to tell you, I hope you won't need my professional services, although I promise you will have them, if you do. But, Tish, can you tell me? What it is you need right now?"

"To be able to keep myself safe," she answered immediately, as if she had been hoping he would ask again, or ask this easier question, as if she had been wanting to tell him that she wasn't safe, so he would take care of it. "I'm sorry," she said, frightened at what she'd said. "I — "

"Safe from what?" he asked. He was keeping his voice calm, but his eyes weren't.

"Tonnie," she said, her eyes watching his face. She didn't know what she was watching for, but she would recognize it when it appeared, and then she would be out of that room, so fast, nobody could catch her for the rest of her life.

The trouble was, it felt so *good* to be saying

it, at last, not to be pretending it never even existed, not even just to be thinking about saying it. *Good* to be free to tell the truth.

She was afraid that if she started, she could never stop.

So she was afraid to start. That made sense.

"Safe from Tonnie," Mr. Battle echoed her. "What is it he does?" The voice, calm — unworried, unfrightened, unanxious — ready for about anything.

Tish ran over in her mind all the things she could say, all the things Tonnie did.

It turned out there wasn't anything she wanted to have to say.

She didn't want to say any of those things.

She was too ashamed of herself.

And Mr. Battle would look at her, then — a way she couldn't stand to be looked at.

The way *everyone* would look at her. Whether they believed her or not. And if it turned out they didn't believe her, Tonnie would really be in position to —

"I can't," Tish said.

She hated her voice, a scared, little-girl voice, the kind of voice that let Tonnie get away with whatever he wanted.

All right, then. Who cared?

So she said it. The easiest, clearest thing, the thing of them all she wouldn't have to explain or describe. She glared at Mr. Battle. "He fucks me."

His face stayed calm. His mouth opened, and Tish almost couldn't hear what he asked. "Don't you mean rapes?"

Ashamed, humiliated, Tish didn't care what he said. She just wanted to get out of there, out of the room where a little piece of the truth had been given a name.

Because she didn't feel free. She felt frightened. If she was starting something and she didn't know what would happen. If she was already not in control of what could happen to her and it was starting to happen.

What was the difference between that, and Tonnie? Nothing, no difference at all.

"Whatever," Tish mumbled. "Anyway, it's late. It doesn't matter," she said. "I have to go — "

"Tish."

He wasn't disgusted. He felt sorry for her. He wasn't turned on by it. He maybe wished he could help her.

"You don't deserve that," he said. And angry, too. "Nobody does, there's no excuse for — " her cheeks flamed hot. "There's nobody who *deserves* it."

He was right, she thought; he was right. She didn't, and nobody did. She should have been able to figure that out. It was stupid of her not to have figured it out, almost as if she wanted to deserve it.

Which maybe she did, since if she deserved it, at least it made some kind of sense. But that made no sense at all, made bad sense, the sense Tonnie wanted her to make out of it.

No more, Tish thought, she wouldn't believe that anymore. So she waited for what Mr. Battle would say next.

He was thinking.

She had her hands up in front of her face, hiding her face.

Eventually, "Since you're eighteen," he said.

Tish didn't know why he thought that.

"You're legally an adult, so you can choose, by law, what you're going to do. About him. If you were underage," Mr. Battle warned her, "the law would require me to — "

"I'm not — " She stopped herself as she figured it out. "I'm eighteen," she said.

"So you can take your time to decide what you want to do about him," Mr. Battle said. "And any time, you just tell me, I'll get to work on charges."

Tish nodded.

"Now, tomorrow, whenever. Do you want to bring charges now?" he asked.

"Please, no, don't," she said. She couldn't *stand* — even the idea of accusing Tonnie in public, and the thought of being asked questions on the witness stand, even just imagining it — She shrank back inside her skin, withering like paper in flames, her heart shriveling up.

"Then what? What do you think we can do? For you, for now. Is it that — Do you want to be able to protect yourself?" Mr. Battle guessed. "Physically?"

She nodded.

"Which is what the knife is for?"

She nodded.

"Well, I'll defend you in court, if that's what happens. If that's why you wanted to see me, what you came for. If that's what you're asking of me."

That wasn't, but "Thank you," she said.

What she was asking was if she was permitted to defend herself, and his answer seemed to be *Yes, but*. Yes, but there will be penalties. Yes, but you're going to get hurt.

Inside Tish a voice screamed in protest, hadn't she already been penalized enough? Hurt enough?

She shut that whining voice up. Because as an answer, *Yes, but* was better than *No.*

"But, Tish," Mr. Battle said.

"What? Go ahead, please tell me, I — "

"Does he know you have the knife?"

"Yes. I — this morning, I showed him. Because I couldn't get to it last night, because it was in a stupid drawer where I hid it." She hadn't meant to say that. She stopped talking. If she was going to start saying things she never meant to say.

"Your mother — ?" he didn't finish the question.

He didn't have to. "She doesn't — I think she convinces herself — "

He didn't say anything else. She started to move again.

"Tish," he said. "Wait." He looked up at her. "I'm thinking," he explained.

She waited. He thought.

After a long time, he said, "All right. All right. Now. Try this: If you write it all down — no, don't be scared, listen — if you write it all down and seal it in an envelope, and I'll date it and sign it across the seal. That way, if anything *does* happen, this will be evidence for you. Or when you decide to bring charges. If you write down now — what happens, and when it started, and how often — "

She couldn't. She couldn't even *say* it.

" — just briefly, if you want, just the basic facts, if you can. So it's there in evidence, if we need it."

We.

"I'd rather not need it, frankly. I'd rather not be defending you against charges of assault, or murder. But there are worse things," Mr. Battle said.

Like ending up hanging from a tree. Like ending up hanging naked from a tree, on your front lawn. Like having that be all you can think of to do with your life.

"Can you tell him that you've talked to me? Are you willing to tell him that you've told a lawyer?" Mr. Battle asked.

Tish could about imagine Tonnie's reaction to that. Her heart beat faster just imagining it, and the backs of her knees felt like — water, like just panels of water, they'd never be able to hold her up —

She shook her head.

" — and tell him you've left a statement here. To let him know — "

"If it frightens him — " Tish whispered.

"You've frightened your stepfather already, haven't you?"

She let that idea into her ears and into her head, and then it sank along down to her stomach.

"A lawyer will frighten him more than a knife, I think," Mr. Battle said. "It'll be more effective."

Tish couldn't argue with that. But she was so afraid —

She'd already started things going. She wished she hadn't, and she was glad she had, but now she didn't know. "I don't have any paper."

"I do. A pad, and you can write on this table, right here. There's no hurry," but he had ripped his top page off the pad, and he moved her chair around for her so she had to sit down at the table. He gave her a blue ballpoint pen and put her lemonade glass where she could reach it, if she wanted a drink of lemonade. Then she heard him go sit on his big leather desk chair, and she heard rustling, as if he was reading papers.

She picked up the pen in her right hand.

She looked at her hand: Just some hand, holding a cheap pen. Some girl's hand. She had nothing to do with that hand. Let that hand do whatever it wanted to.

Her left hand was clenched in her lap, clutching tight onto its own fingers.

Tish put the pen down, and picked up the glass, and got some lemonade into her mouth. Too sweet, and she swallowed.

She picked up the pen again. Wrote the date, on the top right, as if this was some school assignment. She leaned her left elbow onto the table, and grabbed a handful of hair at the back of her head with her left hand. She moved the other hand, with the pen in it, down to line one of the paper.

No, there was no title, so there wasn't anything to go on that top line.

She moved the hand down to the next line, the line with a line below it to rest words on and a line above to keep the letters down to the right size —

I can't, the hand wrote, which felt okay, so she wrote it again on the next line, right below, *I can't do this.*

She moved that hand down another line, and it wrote *I am going crazy* in little, little, tiny little letters.

She didn't dare look at the words she had written. Her left hand came over and took the pen, and wrote — like it was some first-grader who only knew how to make capital letters: HE RAPED ME.

She couldn't believe what she'd written.

Her left hand kept on writing the same thing, over and over, HE FUCKS ME, with a period at the end of each sentence. Then it started writing it like second-grade writing, two lines tall, each small letter half as high as the capital H. Over and over, like a crazy hand that couldn't stop, and she was so tired from the sobbing and jamming her right fist into her mouth to keep the noises into her throat, that she just put her head down on the table, right beside the pad.

And closed her eyes.

Tish woke up. She sat up, afraid.

She'd covered about half a sheet of the long yellow paper with that writing, and Mr. Battle was standing there, looking worried at her, and her nose was running snot all over her mouth and chin. He gave her the box of tissues again.

"Better," she said. That was about all the sound she could get out of her throat.

She started to rip that page off the pad, to start it over, and do it right, but he shook his head. "Just start again, below, I think. Can you trust me in this, Tish?"

She shrugged. It was too late now, anyway.

"You can't expect not to have scars," he said, sad.

Then Tish did laugh out loud, twice. Ha.

169

Ha. He couldn't know — how could he know? — but gaping wounds was more like it, or sores, like untended cancers, oozing blood and pus and the flesh all rotted and collapsed around them, horrible to see, or smell, horrible to have on your body.

"What made you get the knife now, Tish?" Mr. Battle asked. "What changed?"

"Nothing," she said. "I got it so the truth could make me free," she said. "Miranda," she said.

"I SHOULDN'T BE ASHAMED NOT TO BE DEAD!" she yelled.

And then she was ashamed for yelling.

He thought for a minute, and said, "The truth, written down, and a survival knife, and a good lawyer if you need him. I guess you've got a chance. Where will you go?"

"Back there," she realized.

"Then I'm going to ask you to do something for me, Tish," he said. "I want you to telephone me, at eight every morning, at ten every night. Will you do that?"

Tish agreed. She explained, "Because as soon as I don't go back — it'll be because of making charges, and — I don't want always to have been too afraid of him to do anything to help myself, do something myself," she said. And wiped at her eyes with another Kleenex. "You know?"

Mr. Battle looked at her. "Maybe even a pretty good chance," he said. "We have reason to hope," he said.

That was better news than Tish had heard for all of her life.

—Nine—

Tish turned down the offer of a ride. She told Mr. Battle that she wanted to walk so she'd have time to get ready, but she wasn't sure that was true. She thought maybe it was to give herself time to change her mind. She didn't have to tell Tonnie about the paper, and the lawyer. She could get rid of the card in her pocket, with Mr. Battle's office phone number on it, and his home phone number.

She must look pretty funny, clumping along in the Docs and the gym shorts, she thought. She tried to concentrate on how funny she must look, but she couldn't.

Fear grew in her belly, like some speeded-up pregnancy, and shoved up against her heart and vibrated along her bones until she almost couldn't find the leg muscles to keep on walking, clump, clump, back to Tonnie's house.

Thinking about it, it seemed to her better not to say anything to Tonnie. She wouldn't be living there for that much longer anyway, just until she was eighteen. How bad could it be? She already knew how bad it could be, and it wasn't all that bad — was it? She was still around and functioning — wasn't she? So maybe she didn't have to face him. She could just hand over the knife — and then later she'd tell him she was sorry, taking long enough before she finally apologized so he could feel like he'd forced her back where he wanted her, and maybe that would cut short —

The front door was there. Closed.

He was home, his car was parked.

Even standing outside Tish could sense the fury behind that door. She could practically see the door bulging out with all the fury behind it. Waiting for her.

She couldn't change her mind. And she was scared about that, but also glad.

She'd gone too far this morning to go back now.

If she turned back now, and didn't tell him what she'd done, she'd have turned her back on her only chance, on her last chance.

Turned her back on herself.

Even with Mr. Battle on her side, and the paper she'd written her story down on —

No, that wasn't her story. That was just a part of her story. There was more to her than what Tonnie had done, did to her. There was more to her life than the part he was in. He just wanted to take it all away from her; Tonnie wanted to take her whole life away from her.

— folded up, and sealed, and safe in Mr. Battle's office. And the phone calls he was expecting.

If Tonnie killed her, or hurt her so seriously, she couldn't ever tell anyone what he'd done to her, they'd still get him. No matter what, even if she didn't warn him about it, he could no longer do whatever he wanted to her and just get away with it. Not now. Now, no matter what happened to Tish, Tonnie wouldn't get away. Even if he got her before she made up her heart to bring charges. And tell the police.

Because she knew she was going to do that. Sooner or later.

Tish knew it was up to her. She was the only one who could do this first thing, and everything after. She was the one who would have to.

The door waited, bulging with the fury behind it. Once she opened it, and stepped inside — to be swallowed up and thrown around in that fury —

She didn't know if she could make herself open that door.

And go in.

But she didn't have to go inside until she was ready to, Tish thought. Nobody could make her go inside and get away with it, without the neighbors knowing — from the way she would scream and yell for help. So it was up to her to decide when she thought it was okay for her to go in.

She rang the doorbell and then ran back, away from the door. Make Tonnie come out, stand outside, until she'd said her piece, until she had seen in his eyes that the words had gotten into his head.

Outside, Tish knew, standing with her knees locked so she wouldn't fall over, her Docs planted, with the knife in her right boot and words lined up ready to be pushed out of her throat —

In the outside, Tonnie didn't dare act the way he let himself act when he was in his own house.

She looked over her right shoulder, over her left. She felt the emptiness at her back. The whole world, except for Tonnie's house, was the outside.

That was an idea she had never had before. She pictured the whole world — round — like a picture in a book, with the Australians hanging off by their feet and smiling, and the Japanese sticking out of one side, smiling. She pictured how little a dot Tonnie's home made on that globe. Everything except for that tiny little dot *wasn't* his.

All the rest —

Not that she thought the rest of the world was perfect, or even easy, or even safe. Just, it wasn't Tonnie's.

And there was so much of it. So much more of the rest than there ever could be of Tonnie's.

She could almost see how much.

The door started to open, and terror reached out for her, reached up from her belly to grab on to her heart.

Tish wrapped her hand around that picture of how much world stretched out around the few square feet of house that Tonnie owned. She wrapped her hand around the idea and held it out in front of her, like a knife.

ABOUT THE AUTHOR

Cynthia Voigt is a renowned author of books for preteens and young adults. She has written twenty novels, including *Homecoming*, the 1983 Newbery Medal-winner *Dicey's Song*, the 1984 Newbery Honor Book *A Solitary Blue*, and *The Callender Papers*, winner of the Edgar Allan Poe Award. Her most recent book for Scholastic Hardcover is *The Wings of a Falcon*.

Mrs. Voigt lives in Maine with her husband and the younger of her two children.

Designed by Madalina Stefan

Composed by PennSet, Inc.,
Bloomsburg, Pennsylvania,
in Meridien with display type
in Meridien Medium

Printed and bound by Berryville Graphics,
Berryville, Virginia